SPEAKEASY

Visit us at www.boldstrokesbooks.com

By the Author

Shots Fired

Forbidden Passion

Initiation By Desire

Speakeasy

SPEAKEASY

by
MJ Williamz

2015

SPEAKEASY
© 2015 BY MJ WILLIAMZ. ALL RIGHTS RESERVED.

ISBN 13: 978-1-62639-238-0

THIS TRADE PAPERBACK ORIGINAL IS PUBLISHED BY
BOLD STROKES BOOKS, INC.
P.O. BOX 249
VALLEY FALLS, NY 12185

FIRST EDITION: JANUARY 2015

THIS IS A WORK OF FICTION. NAMES, CHARACTERS, PLACES, AND INCIDENTS ARE THE PRODUCT OF THE AUTHOR'S IMAGINATION OR ARE USED FICTITIOUSLY. ANY RESEMBLANCE TO ACTUAL PERSONS, LIVING OR DEAD, BUSINESS ESTABLISHMENTS, EVENTS, OR LOCALES IS ENTIRELY COINCIDENTAL.

THIS BOOK, OR PARTS THEREOF, MAY NOT BE REPRODUCED IN ANY FORM WITHOUT PERMISSION.

CREDITS
EDITOR: CINDY CRESAP
PRODUCTION DESIGN: SUSAN RAMUNDO
COVER DESIGN BY SHERI (GRAPHICARTIST2020@HOTMAIL.COM)

Acknowledgments

First of all, and most importantly, I'd like to thank Dini for her love and support. I'd also like to thank Sarah for her encouragement and belief that this book was worth submitting. Next, I want to thank Speed for taking the time to beta read this for me. And a very special thank you to Bremer for brainstorming with me at the beginning of this endeavor and really helping it take off.

I'd also like to thank Cindy for her editing of my creation and, of course, Rad, for still believing and letting my voice be heard.

Dedication

To Dini—For everything

Chapter One

The August night was hot and sticky, as were the women in the dingy room above the Golden Beaver.

"Come back to bed, baby," the nameless brunette patted the empty spot beside her.

Helen Byrne simply stood at the window, watching the road below.

"In a minute, doll."

"What are you worried about? There ain't no cops anywhere near here."

Helen knew the woman was right. She paid the boys from the West Side well enough to stay away from her speakeasy. But she'd heard there might be federal agents, or Prohis, in town that night. True, they were likely to be more focused on the North Side Gang and their dealings. Or even more likely, on Capone and his endeavors. Still, she refused to be complacent. Sure, she might be small-time compared to them, but she held her own in the underworld of Chicago crime.

She continued to watch the general population walk past the front of the building, which was boarded up to look abandoned. No one gave the place a second glance. The regulars knew to park down the street and walk to the door in the alley. Content that the place was safe, she turned back to her bedmate.

"How long you worked here?" Helen asked her.

"Long enough."

"How come I've never had you before?"

"Maybe I'm always busy when you come by."

Helen nodded. That could be true. The rooms above the speakeasy were frequently all occupied with women servicing johns. The place turned a pretty profit for Helen, who often partook of one of her favorites. None were available that night, so she ended up with the shapely woman lying in front of her.

"What's your name?"

"Polly."

"Not your working name. Your real name."

"Does it matter?"

"Fine. Polly, play with your tits for me."

Polly obliged, cupping her large mounds and squeezing them together before sliding her hands to her nipples, which she pinched and tugged.

Helen loved to watch a woman please herself. The familiar arousal started at her core, and soon her body felt like an oven. Her crotch spasmed as she watched Polly's eyes close in obvious pleasure.

She lowered herself to the mattress and replaced one of Polly's hands with her mouth. She ran her tongue over the taut nipple, lazily licking it while Polly moaned in response.

"You've got a great tongue."

Helen declined to respond, opting rather to close her mouth on the tip of Polly's breast and suck it deep into her mouth. She felt Polly's hand in her hair, pressing her breast to her. She grazed the soft flesh with her teeth while her tongue held the nipple against the roof of her mouth.

Polly wrapped her legs around Helen's thigh and rubbed her wet center against it.

"Baby, I need you to touch me."

"You're kind of impatient, aren't you?"

"You get me hot."

"So enjoy it for a bit."

"Sorry. I'm not used to enjoying it."

"Well, you're not with a john. And you may not have another one tonight. Or you might. It doesn't matter. I don't like to be rushed. I won't be hurried, so rut against me all you'd like, but know I'll fuck you when I'm ready. And not before."

"Damn it, you're powerful. You're so in charge. That gets me wet."

"Stay that way."

Helen moved her mouth to Polly's other breast and kissed around the nipple before taking it in her mouth. She gently ran her tongue around the hard nub while she pinched the other one. The feel of Polly's wet cunt against her leg spurred her on. She loved the raw sexuality of the whore and thought briefly how horrid it must be to spend most of her hours with a cock inside her, rather than in the arms of another woman, which she so obviously preferred.

"Have you always preferred to be fucked by women?"

"You sure ask a lot of questions."

"You sure avoid a lot of answers."

Polly slid her hand between Helen's legs.

"Someone's enjoying herself."

Helen murmured her appreciation as Polly stroked her. She closed her mouth on her breast again and moved her own hand between her leg and Polly's pussy. She ran her fingers over Polly's swollen clit before dipping them inside.

Polly opened her legs and Helen took advantage by plunging deeper inside her.

"You feel so fucking good," Polly said.

Helen continued to thrust in and out of her while she bit down on her nipple and flicked it with her tongue.

Polly took her hand away from Helen and ran her fingers over her own clit.

"You think I need help?" Helen asked.

"I just like the idea of your cream on me."

"Knock yourself out."

Helen climbed between her legs and continued fucking her while she watched her rub her clit. The sight of a woman providing herself pleasure made her hornier than just about anything. She felt her own clit throb while she watched Polly's fingers deftly play.

Polly's breathing became labored. She panted as she arched her hips toward the source of her pleasure. Helen plunged her fingers as deep as she could and held them there, stroking Polly's soft walls with the tips. She felt those walls tremble then close around her as Polly cried out at the force of the orgasm. She waited until the spasms died, then slipped her fingers out.

"I guess my cream on you worked for you, huh?"

"I guess it did."

Polly moved her hand back between Helen's legs as Helen rolled onto her back.

"How come you ain't found some nice dame and settled down?" she asked while she lazily ran her hand over Helen.

"I'm too busy running the show. Besides, no self-respecting Jane would want to be my moll."

"Says you. A gal would have to be crazy not to want to be with a charming, sophisticated woman such as yourself."

"You gunnin' for a tip or something?"

"'Course not. I'm just surprised you ain't got a steady."

"Well, I don't. And I'm not looking. So quit beating your gums and do what you do best."

"I love it when you talk tough."

Helen watched Polly's eyes as they focused between her legs. They widened as Helen's clit grew at her touch.

"Baby, you sure got nice stuff."

"It serves its purpose."

"Yeah, it does." She teased Helen's opening before slipping a finger inside. "You're so hot and wet."

"Fucking a woman does that to me."

"I hope you've got another big come in there for me."

"I'm planning on it."

Helen took Polly's fingers deep, enjoying the fullness. Polly turned her hand and pulled them out before quickly sliding them back in.

"You always watch when you fuck someone?" Helen asked.

"Pussies are beautiful. And it looks hot when yours sucks my fingers in."

Helen was happy Polly was enjoying herself. She didn't like the girls who felt obligated. That was why she had her few that she returned to. She was pretty sure Polly would be added to that list.

She relaxed and let the feelings take over. She was getting wetter with each thrust. Soon her clit felt like it would split from the pressure.

"Rub my clit, doll."

Polly obliged, stroking Helen's clit with her left hand while her right continued its plunging.

The feel of Polly's talented fingers sent Helen teetering. She held on as long as she could, but soon felt the world fall from beneath her and she tumbled into a powerful climax. She felt her cunt close around Polly's fingers over and over as the orgasm continued. When the clenching finally ceased, she lightly grabbed Polly's wrist and pulled her hand away from her clit.

"No more, please."

"Are you a little sensitive?" Polly laughed.

"Just a little."

Polly withdrew her fingers and Helen lay still as she tried to catch her breath.

"You certainly know what you're doing," she said.

"It wasn't my first time."

Helen sat on the edge of the bed and laughed.

"No, I don't suppose it was."

She reached for her clothes and quickly dressed.

"Am I going to see you again?" Polly asked.

"You might," Helen said. She lit a cigarette and fished a twenty out of her money clip. She tossed it on the nightstand. "It's been swell. I'll keep you in mind next time I come around."

She let herself out the door and took the back staircase down to the bar.

Chapter Two

Helen left the oppressively humid air as she ducked in to Mickey O'Leary's. The air was slightly cooler inside. At least it was moving. She stopped to talk to the owner behind the register.

"How's business?"

"Not bad. Kevin's already at your table in the back."

"Thanks. He already pick up the envelope?"

"He did."

"Good. Keep up the good work, Mickey." She turned to walk off.

"You going to have the usual?" he called.

"I am. And don't skimp on the corned beef."

"I wouldn't dream of it."

Helen found Kevin Donegal, her right-hand man, seated by a fan in the back room off the main dining room.

"Sorry I'm late."

"Where you been?"

"Traffic. I don't know where some of those goofs learned to drive."

"You could probably learn to drive a little slower yourself, boss."

Helen stared at Kevin, the twenty-five-year-old farm boy from Omaha who ran away to Chicago when he was barely a teen. They'd been fast friends since they'd worked as sluggers for the Market Street Gang. Paid nicely by the *Tribune,* they beat up any newsboys they caught selling an *Examiner*. It was an easy starting point for a life of crime. The two of them kept an eye out for each other. Although, mostly, it was the wiry Helen making sure the slower, bulkier Kevin was kept safe.

"Says you."

"Says me."

"Are the others coming?"

"They'll be here."

Kevin and Helen always met first, enjoying lunch and discussing the gang before the rest of the lieutenants arrived. They would never speak completely freely in front of the others, but were fairly open with each other.

"How are takes today?"

Kevin handed her several bulky envelopes. She flipped through each one, easily gauging the amount of cash they contained.

"Not bad."

"We're having a good month. People are coming to our area since the other clowns are killing each other right and left."

"No one's been shot for a while," Helen said.

"Still. People are being cautious. It's definitely helping us."

"Did anyone get hit by the Prohis last night?"

"I didn't hear nothing. I don't think they showed."

Helen nodded, but said nothing as Mickey approached with their sandwiches. As usual, she watched with quiet amusement at the way the men looked at each other. She was certain there was more there than a business relationship, but Kevin never brought it up, and she certainly wasn't going to.

"Thanks, Mickey."

"You're welcome, Helen." He seemed to force his focus away from Kevin. "Let me know if you need anything else."

"He's a good egg," Helen said to Kevin.

Kevin shrugged.

"He pays us regular and makes good food."

"That he does."

Helen took a bite of sandwich and sat back as she chewed. The whore's words from the previous night had been bouncing around in her head. She'd been pondering if she should settle down.

"You ever think maybe we're getting too old for this?" she said.

"For what? Making a boatload of money running booze and hookers and protecting businesses?"

"Maybe. Like maybe we should retire or something. Let the young ones run things now."

"Young ones? Too old? You're talking nonsense. I don't see no gray in that auburn hair of yours. What the hell? Where did this bullshit come from?"

"I was just thinking, Kevin. That's all."

"Yeah, well, don't. Not if it means talkin' crazy. Besides, you ain't even thirty yet."

"Not even close."

"We got a lot of years ahead of us. And there's a lot of money to be made."

They finished their sandwiches just as three young men came strolling in, looking nonchalant as they glanced around the place. They all had olive skin and wore their black hair slicked back. The suits they wore were similar to Helen's and Kevin's.

"Who do they belong to?"

"They're with the Outfit."

"What are they doing on our turf?"

Kevin didn't answer and Helen stood, buttoned her sports coat, and casually approached the men.

"Are you boys lost?"

"You Helen Byrne?" a lanky young man with crooked teeth asked.

"Who wants to know?"

His companions drew weapons, but before they could pull their triggers, Kevin had dropped all three with his submachine gun.

"Talk about nerve," he said as he joined Helen over the bodies, his weapon still in his hand as he looked through the window for any others.

"You sure they're from the South Side?"

"Positive." Kevin toed the one who'd approached Helen. "This here's Sal Montero."

The other four lieutenants for Helen's Westside Gang strolled in and stopped when they saw the dead men.

"What happened?"

"Someone tried to hit the boss," Kevin said.

The men drew their weapons and looked around.

"Put those away. It's almost lunchtime here. Get these guys out of here and get this place clean before the crowds come in. Meet us at the barbershop in an hour. And come with answers."

She took the envelope Mickey had given Kevin earlier and withdrew some bills. She handed them to Mickey.

"This should cover any inconvenience."

She motioned to the door and Kevin stepped onto the crowded sidewalk, surveying the scene before he signaled to Helen that it was safe for her to exit. They hurried to his car, and he drove her back to their headquarters behind George's Barbershop."

Neither spoke during the drive. Helen was livid that someone had tried to bump her off in broad daylight at Mickey's. That showed balls and complete disrespect. She admired the gumption, but wouldn't sit to be disrespected like that.

Gangs were a dime a dozen in Chicago. Most of them ignored Helen's gang on the West Side because she was small-time. That wasn't the case with Hymie Weiss's gang in the North or Al Capone's Outfit in the South. They were always taking potshots at Helen and her men.

"So what do we do now?" Kevin asked once they were in the hidden room behind the shop.

"The boys better have some information when they get here. Once we know who was behind it, we get even."

"How?"

"That depends on who it was."

Helen paced until the others arrived.

"Well?"

"Sounds like the order came straight from the top," a young brunette said.

"The top? Why would Capone want to off me?"

"Word is he wanted to use you to send a message to O'Donnell."

Helen nodded. So she wasn't worth taking out as a threat, but only to let another leader know he should back off? She knew she'd have to prove her gang. That was the only type of retaliation that would take some sting off.

"So what are we going to do?" another lieutenant asked.

"Charlie, you and Jack round up ten, maybe fifteen men. I want the First Chicago hit."

"You want us to rob a bank on the South Side?"

"I do. Shoot it up. Take some cash. Get out. I want it quick and clean. And successful."

"When should we do this?"

"Two o'clock."

"That don't give us much time," Jack protested.

"Then you'd better round some fellas up. Don't fuck this up."

Charlie and Jack left, and Helen looked at the remaining three men with her.

"What have you got for me?"

Kevin sat next to Helen while her remaining officers handed over their collections and earnings.

Helen scrupulously entered every amount in a ledger, then split up some money for her men and put the remainder in the safe that only she and Kevin knew the combination to.

One of her men, the oldest at thirty-two, spoke.

"You want us to go keep an eye on the bank in case something goes wrong?"

"Floyd, I trust them. They're in charge. Relax. Pour a drink. Deal some cards. All we do now is wait."

The four of them played poker to pass the time. As usual, Helen was having little trouble relieving the men of their money. Finally, at four o'clock, the door burst open and in walked Charlie and Jack, each lugging hefty bags of cash.

"You did it?"

"We did," Charlie said. "Some fellas gave chase, but we lost them over on the North End. We laid low up there then circled back here."

"Let's see what you brought."

The six of them divvied up the money, and Helen was happy with the take of seven thousand dollars.

"You did good work." She handed the men each a thousand dollars. "This is for all of you. Split it among the men as you see fit."

She locked the rest of the money away and turned to Kevin.

"Take me to get my car, then go get cleaned up. We're going out tonight."

❖

At eight o'clock, Helen slid into the backseat of Kevin's Packard.

"You think they're still gunnin' for you?"

"Beats me, but I'm not taking any chances."

"Where we headed, boss?"

"Gattino's."

"You really are set on getting yourself killed, aren't you?"

"I'm not going to lay low. I need to show them I'm not scared."

"Yeah, but why do we have to go to one of their clubs?"

"I want to check out the competition."

Kevin shook his head, knowing it was useless to argue with Helen once her mind was made up. Instead, he navigated through traffic to the southern edge of Chicago and one of the more famous speakeasies of the city.

They parked several blocks away, and Kevin walked behind Helen, constantly alert for any potential ambush.

"Relax. No one knows I'm going to be here. Hell, you didn't even know until you picked me up."

"Still. We might have had a tail."

"Did you notice a tail?"

"No."

"Then calm down. We'll have to be aware of every movement once we get inside. That will be troubling enough. Don't get all worked up until you have to."

Helen appreciated Kevin and was grateful for his concern. But the last thing she wanted was to call attention to herself as they entered the club. She'd make sure any higher-ups in Capone's organization would know she was there. But she didn't want the general public aware of her. She wanted to observe their establishment, make sure they knew she wasn't backing down, and leave. It would be short and sweet.

They walked in and immediately saw a flurry of activity at a back table. Helen and Kevin reached for their weapons, but neither drew as they approached the bar. Men scattered from the table, leaving one man and a woman.

"Bourbon and water," Helen said.

"Scotch on the rocks." Kevin leaned his large frame against the bar and surveyed the crowd. He quickly noted where each of the men originally at the back table had ended up.

"They're watching us."

"Good. Someone screwed up since I'm still alive. They're probably all worried about the wrath of Big Al."

"They really fucked that hit up."

"They underestimate us. Big mistake."

She turned her attention to the table at the rear of the club. She easily recognized Franco Moretti from her teen gang years. She raised her glass to him, but he simply sat staring at her.

"Shall we say hello?"

"Lead the way."

As they cut through the crowd, Helen's focus was drawn away from Moretti to the dark beauty sharing his table. She stopped briefly as she looked at the woman she'd seen many times on the arms of many lower ranking officers. She looked striking sitting with Franco, like she was on top of the world where she belonged.

The woman's gaze never left Helen as they approached. Helen knew she should look at Franco, but she didn't give a shit. They'd disrespected her. She could disrespect him.

She drew her eyes away from the Italian beauty only when she was standing at the table. She looked at Capone's lieutenant and smiled.

"How's things, Moretti?"

"Helen. Nice of you to stop by. Have a seat."

His words were flat, his tone carefully measured. Helen walked around the table so her back was also to the wall. She sat next to Moretti's girl while Kevin stood behind her.

Helen turned her attention to the woman.

"Maria, isn't it? You've certainly fucked your way up the ranks, haven't you?"

Maria placed a cigarette between her painted lips, and Helen was quick to light it. She'd never seen her up close before, and found herself appreciating her lined brown eyes and red lips.

Maria took a long drag on her cigarette and exhaled in Helen's face. She turned to Franco.

"I'm bored."

"Maybe what you need is someone like me who can show you what a good time really is," Helen said. She heard Kevin snicker behind her.

"You here to talk to me or her?" Franco asked.

"I'm just here for a drink." Helen leaned back and surveyed the crowd.

"You don't belong here. I'm sure you think you had some point to make. Now you can beat it."

"I'm just getting warmed up."

"Franco, baby, I'm bored," Maria whined again.

"Come on, doll." Helen stood and offered her hand. "Let's dance."

"With you?"

"I don't see anyone else offering."

Maria pouted at Franco, who stared silently at Helen.

"Are you gonna make me dance with *her*?"

"What do I care?"

Maria stood and deliberately turned away from Helen as she moved to the floor. A jazz ensemble was playing a catchy number. Helen pulled Maria to her and they began to move. Helen considered herself an expert dancer and was pleasantly surprised that Maria kept pace. By the end of their second dance, Maria was laughing and obviously enjoying herself.

Helen felt something shift inside as they danced to a third song. She enjoyed watching Maria move and wondered how she'd move in bed. Her desire had moved from wanting to stick it to Franco to honestly wanting to make time with Maria.

Exhausted after three songs, they walked back to the table, Helen with her arm easily draped over Maria's thin shoulders.

"How tall are you?" Maria asked, looking up at Helen.

"I'm five eight."

"I'm only five three. No wonder you seem bigger than life."

"I'm tall, all right. Bigger than life? Sometimes, maybe." She grinned.

"This one can really cut a rug." Maria laughed as she fell into her seat. She reached for her drink, only to find her glass empty. She turned to Franco and pouted again.

"I'll get you a refill, doll." Helen stood. "You want another one, Moretti?"

"I'm fine."

Helen pushed through the crowd with Kevin at her back.

"You trying to see how mad you can make him?" he asked. "What happened to getting in and getting out?"

"I'm having fun."

"She's Moretti's girl. You can't really be thinking of fucking her."

"She's a smarty. And you know she's got to be ripe for some real bedtime."

"You've made your point, Helen. We don't need to push your luck."

"Right. We'll leave after these drinks."

They got back to the table and Maria's mood had noticeably soured.

"What's wrong?" Helen asked.

Maria didn't say anything.

"Hey, I thought we were having some laughs. What happened?"

"I'm not supposed to have fun with you."

"Why not?"

"Leave her be," Franco said. "You've stayed longer than you needed. I'm sure you have business to attend."

Helen didn't like feeling like she was getting the bum's rush, but the hardened look in Franco's eyes told her she was testing her good fortune.

"Maria." She bent over Maria's hand and brushed the knuckles with her lips. She extended a hand to Franco, who didn't move.

"You've made your point," he said. "I suggest you keep away from our territory from now on."

"It's a small town."

"Not that small."

"I'm sure I won't see any of your friends in my neighborhood, either?"

"I wouldn't think so." His eyes never softened. She knew she'd never believe him, but the words sounded good.

"Nice seeing you again." She winked once more at Maria and led Kevin out into the muggy night air.

Chapter Three

Work had kept Helen busy, and tensions between gangs ran high. She needed some downtime and a little relief. She knew she could hire a working girl for the night, but she was in the mood for the chase, the game of wooing a young lady to share her bed. She drove to Towertown, or what was left of the art colony on the Near North Side.

She parked under the giant water tower that gave the neighborhood its name and walked the busy streets, admiring the gays and lesbians enjoying the September night. She made her way to The Corset, a speakeasy specifically for women who loved women. She smoothed her jacket and adjusted her tie. She may not have literally owned the place, but that wouldn't stop her from acting like she did.

She sauntered in and looked around. Damn, she loved flappers. She loved tits, to be sure, but there was something alluring about the boyish look of a flapper, with their flattened chests and straight waists. She liked the game of a dame peeking out from under the brim of her hat with charcoal around her eyes.

While she very much enjoyed her own hair bobbed, she missed the days the ladies' hair fell to their waists. Still, she couldn't deny her love of this new breed of women.

She watched a few couples on the dance floor shimmying and shaking while the band played. She noted several women at tables throughout the room who were focused on her. She leaned against the bar and weighed her options as she waited for the bartender.

A small blonde walked up to her. She couldn't have been more than five feet tall, but there was a spunk to her step and a challenge in her gaze.

"You're Helen Byrne, ain't ya?"

Helen was awash with conflicting emotions. While she enjoyed her notoriety and sense of fame, sometimes she just wanted to be another nameless person out looking for a good time. This was one of those times.

"What do you know about Helen Byrne?"

"I work at the orphanage on Wabash."

Helen cringed at the mention of her childhood home.

"What's your point?"

"I know you drop off things for the kids all the time. Like blankets and warm clothes in the winter."

"That's what you heard, huh?"

"I've seen you."

It was true. Helen really felt for the kids at the orphanage and knew they never had enough. She also knew if she gave the place money, the priests that ran it would pocket every last cent. So she bought supplies and dropped them off herself, making sure they got to the kids.

"Sure. That's me."

"Well, it's a pleasure to finally meet you. I have to say you're quite a legend."

"I'd think workin' at an orphanage and all that, you'd be a law-abiding citizen and not be able to stand the likes of me."

"Why? Because you're a bootlegger? Prohibition is a stupid law. I'd have to think so or I wouldn't be here, right?"

"Good point."

Helen was amused by the spry woman. She looked soft and kind, but there was a definite edge to her.

"Can I buy you a drink?"

"I'll have a martini."

She took the drink from Helen, who studied her another moment.

"I thought only nuns worked at the orphanage."

"Yeah. So?"

Helen choked on her drink.

"You're a nun?"

"I am. My name's Mary Margaret. You can call me Maggie."

"Wouldn't the mother superior be a little upset if she knew where you were?"

"Sure she would. But she'll never know."

Helen motioned to an empty table and admired the sway of Maggie's hips as she followed her.

"You dance?" Helen asked.

"Doesn't everyone?"

Helen stood and offered her hand, which Maggie took. She led her to an open spot on the floor and they proceeded to dance the Charleston. The band played many lively tunes, and Helen was more than happy to continue dancing with the energetic Maggie.

"You sure know how to cut a rug," Helen said when they finally sat down again.

"You're not so bad yourself. Where did you learn to dance like that?"

Helen shrugged. She'd picked up moves watching the older guys from the gangs at the bars when she was coming up the ranks. She didn't think that sounded all that impressive.

"I think maybe I was just born with it."

"That happens. Well, you're sure a natural."

"So tell me, Sister. How does a nun learn of a speakeasy in Towertown?"

"I listen. I learn."

"But good, Mass-going people don't frequent this area of town."

"No, but when places like this get raided, they talk about it. A lot."

Helen nodded.

"True. So you hear about it, then lay low and check it out when the heat's died down."

"Exactly."

Helen smiled at Maggie's cleverness and raised her glass to her before taking a sip.

"So tell me everything there is to know about who Helen Byrne really is."

Helen leaned back in her chair and crossed her ankle over her knee.

"There's not much to tell."

"I think you're swell. I think it's great that you haven't forgotten where you came from and you give back some of what you make."

"I'm flattered. But I don't feel like I do anything special. I just try to do what's right."

"More people should follow your lead."

"You're an interesting person, Sister Mary Margaret. There's a bit of a pious side to you, even as you sit here sipping an illegal martini with a known rumrunner."

"I suppose I come across as pious only because I do believe in helping the less fortunate. As for the rest of it, I'm enjoying a drink with an attractive woman. That would be the human side of me."

Helen leaned forward and traced Maggie's jaw.

"I like the human side of you."

"There's plenty of it for you to see."

Helen arched an eyebrow.

"How much are you willing to show me?"

"The sky's the limit."

"I keep an apartment a few blocks away."

"Lead the way."

Helen reached for Maggie's hand and led the way out of the bar and down the street to a newer building. She let them in and rode the elevator to the eighth floor. Her apartment covered the west side of the floor and had an expansive view of the city.

"This is nice." Maggie was visibly impressed. "How many other places like this do you have?"

"I have a few." Helen went to the bar while Maggie looked around. She mixed a martini, then poured her usual bourbon and water.

She found Maggie in the library.

"Have you read all these books?" Maggie asked.

"Not all, but most. Someday I'll have them all read."

"But there must be a million."

"I enjoy reading."

"You're an interesting person, Helen Byrne. A street thug who reads."

Helen threw her head back and laughed loudly.

"A street thug, huh? Is that all I am?"

"Well, you're the leader of a criminal organization, it's true. But you're still just a thug, aren't you?"

"I suppose I am."

"I don't mean any disrespect."

Helen grabbed Maggie and pulled her close.

"I didn't take it that way." She lowered her mouth and tasted Maggie's. She tasted the martinis as their lips met tentatively. She straightened.

"That's all I get?" Maggie asked.

"You in some kind of hurry?"

Helen looked into Maggie's eyes and saw them darkened with need. She bent again, running her tongue over Maggie's lips until they opened, inviting her in. She lazily traced Maggie's tongue until her own need overwhelmed her. She pressed her mouth hard against Maggie, plunging her tongue urgently deeper.

Maggie leaned against Helen, who was frustrated at her inability to fully feel the swell of her breasts.

Helen stepped back and spun Maggie. She deftly unzipped her dress and loosened her Side Lacer, peeling away the confining garment and coddling her pert breasts as they sprung free.

"Who the hell invented these things?" She nuzzled the back of Maggie's neck.

Maggie fell back against her.

"It's all the rage."

"Still, I'd prefer easier access."

She gently turned Maggie around and kissed her while her hands continued to cup her breasts, her thumbs lightly caressing the hardened nipples.

"That feels so good," Maggie moaned.

Helen guided Maggie into her bedroom and eased her onto the bed. She placed Maggie's legs over her own shoulders and peeled down her stockings. She kissed the inside of her ankle and moved her mouth up her sleek calf to the back of her knee. Turning, she did the same to the other leg.

Maggie squirmed, arching her hips at Helen's ministrations. Helen lowered Maggie's legs and slid her panties off. She stripped her own clothes off and lay on top of her. She kissed her hard as her hands made their way back to Maggie's breasts. They were small but firm and fit perfectly in her hands.

She replaced her hands with her mouth and teasingly licked around one, then the other hardened nipple. She loved how responsive her nipples were and finally sucked one deep inside her mouth.

Maggie cried out as Helen twirled the exposed nipple between her thumb and finger. She traded nipples then, still making sure they both received attention. Maggie was writhing on the bed beneath her. She brought her knee up and pressed it into her. She groaned at the warm wetness she met.

Helen kissed down Maggie's soft belly until she reached the source of that heat. She ran her tongue over her hard clit before dipping it inside. She licked as deep as she could, reveling in the sweetness that was Maggie. She moved back to her clit and sucked and licked it while she plunged her fingers inside her.

Maggie was bucking against her, meeting every thrust, until her body froze, her hand pressed against the back of Helen's head. She cried out then collapsed back on the bed.

Helen lay against her and was surprised when Maggie rolled on top of her. She spent little time on Helen's small breasts as she kissed her way between her legs. She moved her tongue all over Helen, eliciting guttural cries. She didn't stop until Helen gasped and stilled, feeling the rush of the orgasm as it flowed through her.

❖

"The Northsiders took out some cops last night," Kevin said as he entered headquarters the next day.

"How did that happen?"

"They were going after some of Hillyer's men. The police were responding to another call over on the East Side and got caught in the crossfire."

"Anyone we know?"

"They took out Jimmy DeSoto and Carl Olveira."

"No shit?" Helen recognized the names of two top officers of the East Side. "The guys from the Outfit have to be happy to see them go."

"I'm not sure who the hits helped more. But it seems like both gangs are trying to eliminate the outsiders."

"And we're outsiders."

"We are."

As if on cue, the staccato of gunfire sounded against the walls outside. Kevin threw Helen on the ground and fell on top of her.

Helen waited for her heart to beat normally again before nudging Kevin to get off of her.

"Fuckers."

"Shit. That was a waste of bullets." Kevin moved toward the door.

"Don't open that."

"They're not out there. I heard them speed off. I just want to see how bad the place got tattooed."

"Listen to me. It could be a setup. Just cool your heels."

They sat tensely in the windowless back room, their breathing the only sound for half an hour. They finally heard a car pull up and heard the engine turn off.

"You think they're back?" Kevin asked.

"It could be some of ours."

They listened to three car doors slam closed, then the unmistakable sound of a tommy gun.

"Fuck, boss."

The sound of squealing tires filled the immediate quiet.

Helen's heart sank. She and Kevin stared at each other. They needed to see who'd been taken out.

"Careful when you open that door."

Kevin nodded and stood back as he turned the knob.

When no shots rang out, Kevin stepped into the early autumn air.

Helen held back, dreading a sound she didn't know how she'd handle. Fortunately, the afternoon was quiet, so she followed Kevin and found him standing over the lifeless body of young Jack and two of his buddies who were trying to move up the ranks of her gang.

"Shit!"

"They were just kids," Kevin said.

"It happens."

Crowds were gathering across the street as people emerged from their offices to witness the latest carnage in the rum wars.

"I hate that they get to see the guys like this," Kevin said.

"I'll call Flander's. You get some sheets."

Helen phoned her connection at the funeral home and was happy the van showed up before the cops. They had the bodies removed, and Kevin and Helen were sitting in the barbershop when police finally arrived.

"Miss Byrne?" Bobby Turnell, a favorite cop of Helen's, walked in. "Do you know what happened back behind this shop?"

"I heard there was some commotion, but I didn't see anything."

"We heard something about bodies," the greenhorn with him said.

"Did you see any?" Helen asked pointedly.

"Miss Byrne," Bobby said, "this is Officer Dunston. He's new on the force."

Helen sized up the young man. She'd catch up with Turnell later to see how to grease the new man.

"Nice to meet you." Helen extended her hand.

"I've heard of you," Dunston said.

"All good things, I hope."

He didn't respond, and Helen looked at Bobby, who simply said, "Time's about up here."

Helen and Kevin exchanged a knowing look. Dunston would have to go. Bobby had used their code phrase. Helen made a mental note to make it happen quickly.

The police left and Helen called the other lieutenants to round up some men to fix up the outside of headquarters.

"Let's head to the Beaver," Helen said to Kevin. "I could use a drink."

The speakeasy was still closed when they arrived. Kevin went behind the bar and grabbed a couple of bottles, one of Scotch and one of bourbon. He joined Helen at a table and poured the booze.

"What are you thinking?" he asked.

"We don't know who killed the boys today."

"What's your gut say?"

"I want to believe it was some of Weiss's men."

"What do we do?"

"I hate to say it, but I think we need to talk to the Outfit about getting some protection."

"That could get expensive."

Helen sipped her drink as she pondered the consequences of her idea.

"It could. And who's to say we could trust them?"

"I could see them taking our money and still trying to eliminate us. I don't know, boss. I'm not crazy about this notion."

"We can't hold them both off. They're better equipped."

"Maybe we should just lay low for a while."

"You're saying you want to give up? What? Just close up shop? Seems to me I mentioned doing that last month and you called me nuts."

"We've been recruiting and expanding. I'm just saying we should take it back to our area for a spell and let things cool down."

"Will they ever cool down? That's my worry. I don't know that they'll stop until it's just the two organizations."

They each reached for their weapons when they heard someone at the door, but relaxed to see it was Joe, the bartender.

"You two about scared the shit out of me!"

"Sorry," Helen said.

"Everything okay?"

"Sure."

"I'm going to start setting up. If you need anything, give a yell."

"Don't mind us. We won't be staying long."

"Where are we going?" Kevin asked when Joe had retreated to the office.

"I think we need to go back to Gattino's."

"Are you not thinking clearly? Moretti told us to scram and not come back."

"We need to go back."

"Why?"

"I need to get a feel from Franco. I should be able to tell if they were behind today's activity."

"Shit, boss. If they wasn't before, they'll sure as shit make a move on us now if we tread on their turf again."

"You worry too much, Kevin."

Chapter Four

Helen was all business when she and Kevin entered Gattino's. She watched the men scramble from the table against the far wall again, then headed straight back. Kevin followed close behind.

"We need to talk, Moretti." She nodded at Maria, who looked stunning in a red spaghetti-strapped number. "Beat it, doll. I need some alone time with your man."

"She ain't goin' anywhere." Moretti's voice was like ice. "She only takes orders from me."

"Speaking of orders, who gave the one this afternoon?"

"I don't know what you're talking about."

"Bullshit." Helen gazed around the room and saw she was the focus of many men, most of whom had itchy trigger fingers. She pulled a chair around and sat next to Moretti.

"Look, I don't want any trouble from the Outfit. You gotta know that."

Moretti merely shrugged.

"I want to know if it came from the Northsiders. What do you say? Just finger them for me."

"You got a problem with Weiss? Take it up with him. Don't be sullying my bar with talk of those amateurs."

"I know he shot up some of the Eastenders. Hillyer's gotta be pissed. I say we let them fight it out. That will leave more for us. It doesn't make sense for you guys to be gunning for me."

"I told you. I don't know what you're talking about."

"Says you. Fine. Just tell Al we don't want any trouble with him."

"You sayin' you're scared? Why not just close shop then?"

"We're small potatoes, Franco. We're not takin' any money from you."

"You ain't givin' us any money, neither. You want to pay for some protection or something? Fine, I'll talk to Mr. Capone."

"We don't need protection. I just thought we could reason this out. Obviously, I was wrong."

She stood and nodded to Maria who looked positively bored.

"I'm sorry this wasn't more of a social call, lovely lady."

Maria rolled her eyes.

"You look beautiful tonight. You should be on someone's arm who can really show you off."

"You're pushing it, Byrne," Moretti said.

Helen couldn't suppress a smile as she cut through the crowd and left the speakeasy.

"What the hell was that?" Kevin asked. "You even had me believing you was gonna ask for protection."

"I told you I wouldn't do that. And I won't. We'll do what you said. We'll hold steady and not expand for a while. At least until the heat's died down a little bit."

Kevin drove Helen back to the Beaver. The place was jumping, and Helen's mood finally lifted slightly.

"You goin' upstairs tonight?" Helen teased him. In all their years together, she'd never known Kevin to use a prostitute. It was just one more thing that made her wonder again about her first lieutenant and Mickey.

"Nah. I'm good. You?"

"I think I'm okay for now. I just want to relax."

The evening passed uneventfully as they listened to the music and chatted up the customers. Helen even danced a few dances. It was getting late when Helen saw her walk through the back door. Helen stood slowly, unsure of what to make of the situation. She motioned to Kevin, who quickly and quietly alerted other gang members to be on alert.

Helen crossed through the crowd and laid a hand on Maria's fur-covered shoulder.

"Maria? You lost?"

Maria turned with her drink and shrugged. "I'm just bored."

Helen saw several of her men slip outside to check for interlopers. But she kept her focus on Maria, whose eyes lit up when their gazes met.

"You don't look so bored."

"I am."

"I can't believe Franco let you out of his sight."

Maria shrugged again. "We had a fight."

Helen was still wary of a setup, but found it hard to resist the best girl of one of Al Capone's top men. She slipped her arm around Maria.

"Come here and tell me all about it." She led her to her table. "What were you two fighting about?"

"We always do the same thing. It never changes. We don't mix it up at all. We go to that dumb bar and sit there night after night. I told him even you go to different bars sometimes."

Helen fought a smile. It was nice to think of Maria throwing her name out at Moretti.

"That's always business, though, doll. Your guy and I aren't that different."

"You don't see him here. He never goes anywhere the Outfit doesn't own."

"And just what do you think he'll do when he finds out you were here?"

"Who says he's going to find out?"

Helen nodded slowly. She didn't think that was likely, but she admired Maria's guts.

Helen's men had made their way back into the speakeasy and nodded to her that the coast was clear. Maria's story checked out. She appeared to be there alone.

"As long as you're here, what do you say we dance a little?"

Maria shrugged. "Might as well."

Helen couldn't suppress a laugh.

"If you're looking for a good time, doll, you've come to the right place. If you're really that bored, why don't you beat it?"

"You gonna talk or dance?"

Still chuckling, Helen took Maria's hand and led her to the floor. They danced easily for several songs, until they were both tired and made their way back to their table.

"You move really well," Maria said.

"So do you." Helen had given up denying her attraction to Maria. She wanted her and she wanted her soon. The trick would be to see if Maria was interested.

They sipped their drinks, and soon the ensemble slowed their tempo, and Helen couldn't resist the chance to hold Maria. She stood and offered a hand.

"What do you say?"

"Why not?"

Suddenly, the background noise was muted, the cacophony hushed as Helen returned to the dance floor with Maria. She was aware of nothing but the beauty of Maria, the pounding of her own heart, and the pulsing between her legs.

Helen slid her hand around Maria's waist and pulled her close. She took Maria's hand in hers and deftly led her in time with the music. She noted, not for the first time, the scent of her perfume. It was subtle yet heady, smelling of spice and leather, and left Helen dizzy with desire.

"You sure smell swell," she said.

"Thanks. It's Tabac Blond."

"You don't say. Well, I like it."

Maria smiled but said nothing else. Helen searched her mind for another topic of conversation but came up empty. She guided Maria around the floor in silence. Every move, every brush against each other, fueled the fire in Helen. She was aching from the need to have Maria. And Maria seemed to be enjoying herself. She moved easily at Helen's direction and never pulled away from the contact Helen initiated. Helen was thinking she might actually get her to bed, when Maria pulled away.

"I've got to get going."

"What? You just got here," Helen said.

"No, I've been here too long. I'd better get home. I'll see you around."

Helen was left standing in the middle of the dance floor as she watched Maria grab her wrap and flee out the back door.

❖

The next morning, Helen took a group of men to the North Side with intentions to hit some men on the street. They drove through the streets, in the general vicinity of the flower shop the rival gang used as headquarters. As they drove past a deli not far from the shop, they spotted a group of Hymie's men. Helen opened fire first and the others followed. They felled the men and sped off, hurrying off to meet at the Beaver.

Kevin was waiting for them.

"I wish I could have been part of that," he said.

"No way we both could have been there. If they'd retaliated, one of us has to be elsewhere, just in case."

"So how'd it go?"

"We got about six or seven of them."

"Good job."

"Pour some drinks," Helen called to one of her lieutenants.

The booze flowed freely as they celebrated their retaliation.

Helen sipped her bourbon, ever vigilant for the sound of cars outside. After a couple of hours, she decided it was safe for them to leave.

"Head out now and get to work. But be safe out there. I don't want to lose any more of you. Be aware of everything going on around you and report any trouble to me. Now get going."

Chapter Five

The roads were covered with snow and it was still coming down hard. Helen was in a foul mood when she reached the barbershop.

"People need to learn to drive in this damned weather," she said as she shook out of her coat and untied her scarf. "I swear to God, it's not that hard."

She paused as she hung her jacket on the rack. "What's up, Kevin? You look like you're about to bust over there."

"You ain't gonna believe what happened."

"So try me."

"Weiss and Moran took a shot at Capone and Torrio last night."

"You don't say. Bugsy Moran and Hymie Weiss. The tops of the North going after the tops of the South? Well, don't that beat all? So did they get either of them?"

"No. But they shot up their car but good. Torrio's driver is dead."

"Maybe it's time to quit laying low, huh, Kevin? We'll let them take out each other and we'll just keep upping our business over here on the West."

"That's just what I was thinking, boss."

"Are the others coming or what?"

"They know we have a meeting this afternoon. I imagine they might be late with this storm."

"They'd better know how to drive in it. Unlike the rest of the sissies out there."

Kevin laughed as he poured a cup of coffee.

"You want some, boss?"

"I'm good."

He opened his flask and liberally added to his coffee.

"We need to celebrate," Helen said.

"I am." Kevin toasted her with his coffee cup.

"No." Helen laughed. "I mean a real celebration. Let's have Joe open up the Beaver early today."

"Sounds good to me."

The rest of her lieutenants showed up and Helen shared the good news with them.

"Each of you need to take on more business," she said. "I want a new business paying protection from each of you by next month. And, Louis, I want you to look into more booze coming in from Canada. Marty, I want specs for a new speakeasy by the middle of next month. I want to be ready to take advantage of the war between the North and the South. I guarantee they'll forget about us for a while."

"Now on to the important business." Kevin stood. "The boss says we're partying today. Let's all head to the Beaver."

"Did you call Joe?" Helen asked.

"I did. He should be ready by now."

"Bring some of the other guys, too," Helen said. "Let's make this a real shindig."

The men dispersed with much merriment. Helen herself felt more at ease than she had in months.

"I'm glad we're taking on more business," Kevin said when they were alone again. "I think the guys were getting restless."

"Who wasn't? But we had to cool our heels. Now we can get back to business and let Weiss and Capone take each other out. They'll be too busy to give us a second thought. Mark my words."

Helen rode with Kevin to the Golden Beaver.

"I'm pretty happy about getting a new juice joint going," Kevin said.

"You've got something against the Beaver?"

"Not a thing. But it will be fun to have another place to hang out."

"That it will. It'll mean a lot of work to get it up and running, you know."

"Sure. Where are you thinking of opening it?"

"We'll see what Marty comes up with. I've thought about this for a while. I have a few ideas, but I want to see what he says."

They parked blocks from the speakeasy and hurried through the snowstorm to the alley and inside the bar. Several of the guys were already there, drinking and laughing and enjoying their impromptu day off.

Helen bought a round and settled into her seat at the back where she could watch the comings and goings. She was antsy, even though she was happy. She told herself she'd have a few drinks then take the edge off with a girl upstairs. It had been a while since she'd partaken.

The afternoon turned to evening and Helen was excusing herself to go upstairs when the door burst open and in walked Franco Moretti with Maria on his arm and three goons in tow.

Kevin was up in a shot and stood with his hand on his gun. Moretti cut through the crowd and approached Helen, who was determined to be unflappable.

"Franco, welcome to the Golden Beaver. Can I buy you a drink?"

"Get me a Scotch and a red wine for her," Moretti said to one of his henchmen. He turned back to Helen. "No, thank you."

"To what do we owe this pleasure?" Helen spoke to Franco, but never took her eyes off Maria, who looked decidedly uncomfortable.

Moretti pulled two chairs over and waited until Maria sat and then sat next to Helen. He waited until their drinks arrived to speak.

"I suppose you heard about what happened," he said as his gaze focused on the crowd around them.

"Yeah, terribly scary. Lucky Big Al wasn't hit."

"I'm here to make sure you know what a foolish thing that was."

"I heard Hymie and Bugs were behind that. Surely you didn't think it was us."

"Says you. If we find out it was you, you're in for it."

"We had nothing to do with that and you know it," Helen said. "If you're here to mix things up, then just leave now. We aren't looking for trouble tonight."

"Looks like everybody from your gang is here. Seems to me like maybe you're celebrating something."

"We had nothing to do with that hit. And if we did, why would we celebrate? No one got taken out."

"Still, don't get any ideas."

"What? You think I'll put a hit on Al and Johnny? You think I've got a death wish?"

"Good. Remember that."

Helen was pissed at Franco and needed to work off some steam. The sight of Maria in a black Georgette dress did little to ease her pressure. She finally stood and offered her hand to Maria.

"Come on. Let's dance." She glanced at Moretti. "Is that okay with you?"

"Like I care."

"I don't feel like dancing." Maria looked away from Helen, who was confused by her apparent disdain.

"What's up, doll?"

"Nothing. I just don't want to dance right now."

"Come on. You know you're bored sitting there. Let's cut a rug."

"She said she don't want to," Moretti said.

"Fine. Fine." Helen sat down, a bundle of nerves. She wanted Franco and Maria and their thugs out of there so she could go upstairs and relieve some tension. She wasn't happy when Franco sent a goon back to the bar for refills.

"Baby, I'm bored," Maria finally whined to Franco.

"So dance with Helen."

"I don't want to."

"Then shut your trap."

Maria looked over at Helen. "You still offering to dance with me?"

"Any time, doll."

"Fine. Let's dance." She sounded resigned, rather than excited, which confused Helen even more. They'd had some good times together. What was her problem?

They found a spot on the dance floor and began to move with the rhythm.

"What's eating you, doll?" Helen said in her ear.

"I said I wanted to dance, not talk."

"I don't get it. We've had some laughs. Now you're not speaking to me? What gives?"

Maria stormed off the dance floor and sat next to Franco, turning away from Helen. Helen was tired of Maria's attitude, so quickly grabbed another gal to dance with. When she finally got back to the table, Franco was finishing his second drink.

"I think our work here is done," he said.

"Come back any time." Helen's voice dripped sarcasm.

Franco shot her a look as he stood. "You just mind yourself. Remember that."

"You got it."

Franco crooked his arm and Maria slipped her hand in his elbow. They left with their henchmen following.

Helen quickly made her way upstairs. She knocked on the door of Katherine, one of her usuals. The door was opened by a curvy brunette in a red camisole.

"Hey, you," she purred. "Come on in."

Helen slipped the Do Not Disturb sign on the doorknob and walked over to the bed. As she sat down, Katherine handed her a bourbon and water.

"Thanks, doll."

Katherine sat next to her, rubbing her full breasts against Helen.

"It's been too long, baby."

"Yeah, it has."

Katherine turned Helen so she could massage her shoulders.

"You're tense, baby. Everything okay?"

"Sure. You know. Business as usual."

She continued kneading her shoulders and back until Helen put her drink down and shifted to face Katherine. She ran her hands over her soft shoulders and arms, bringing them to rest on her breasts. She ran her thumbs over the hard nipples poking at her.

"You sure know how to make a dame feel good," Katherine moaned.

"Yeah? That's good to hear," she said. "You been busy tonight?"

"You're my first."

"That's even better to hear."

She stood and loosened her tie, then unbuttoned her shirt.

"Here, let me help you," Katherine said.

She untucked Helen's shirt and eased it back over her shoulders. She lifted her undershirt over her head and bent to kiss the small breasts laid bare for her. Helen stood stoic as she felt Katherine's hands deftly unbutton her slacks, then lower her zipper. She stepped out of her trousers and boxers and lay on the bed.

"Come over here, doll."

Katherine straddled Helen and rubbed her wetness along her belly.

"Mm, you feel good," Helen murmured.

Katherine took a nipple in her mouth and played her tongue over it before moving to the other and doing the same thing. Helen felt her clit swell as Katherine's tongue worked its magic. Her breath caught as Katherine released her nipple and kissed down her belly. When she was between her legs, Helen spread them wide and closed her eyes, lost in the feelings Katherine was creating.

Katherine licked around her opening before sucking her swollen lips. Helen arched her back, craving more of what Katherine offered. Katherine moved her tongue to Helen's clit and circled it several times before taking it in her mouth. Helen gasped at the sensation, her head reeling with need.

Helen pressed Katherine into her and moved against her talented mouth. Katherine reached a hand up and pinched Helen's nipple. That was all it took. Helen cried out as the orgasms cascaded over her, each one stronger than the other until they finally stopped.

"You did good, doll," Helen said when Katherine was lying next to her. She ran her hand under Katherine's camisole and fondled a large breast. "I like what you offer."

"It's all yours, baby."

Helen pushed the straps off Katherine's shoulders, exposing the breasts to her. She took one in her mouth, while she rolled the other between her finger and thumb. She moved her hand lower and found Katherine wet and ready for her. She quickly buried three fingers inside her and began to move them in and out. Faster and faster she plunged, with Katherine bucking against her, meeting each thrust.

Helen ran her thumb along Katherine's clit, and Katherine screamed her name as she rode the orgasm to its finish.

"Thanks for that, boss lady."

"My pleasure." Helen downed the rest of her drink and got dressed.

"Don't stay away so long next time," Katherine said.

"I won't." Helen threw some bills on the nightstand and strolled back downstairs to the party.

Chapter Six

The middle of February arrived, and Helen sat with her lieutenants to discuss the building of the new speakeasy. The tensions were still high between the Northsiders and the Outfit in the South, with another blatant attempt on Johnny Torrio's life. Helen knew it was the right time to start moving ahead.

"What have you found out, Marty?"

"We found a great location up north a ways. Just off Twenty-Second Street. It's a prime spot. I've got a crew ready to get started as soon as you say go."

"Twenty-second? That sounds like a good area," Kevin said.

"Let's go take a look," Helen said.

They loaded into the Packard and drove through town until they reached the boarded up former shoe shop on Twenty-second. Helen got out and walked around back, pleased to see the alley would present a perfect entrance. She glanced around and didn't see anything that belonged to either Capone or Weiss.

"Get busy renovating this place. I want it open soon. Then we'll start offering protection to the nearby businesses. This could be a gold mine. Good job, Marty."

Helen was happy as she and Kevin drove back to the barbershop. When they arrived, they found Saul, one of their younger members, looking distraught.

"What's going on?" Helen asked.

"Someone beat up Manny and Tiger really bad."

"Wait. What?"

"They were shaking down some people up Archer a ways. Some goons jumped them and beat them up pretty good."

"Where are they?"

"They took them to the Chicago General."

"Shit. Who did it?"

"I don't know. I got there right after it happened."

"Why weren't you with them?" Helen demanded.

"I was working a couple blocks over."

Helen nodded. That seemed plausible. At least he hadn't been with them and run away. She was sick that some of the youngsters had been hurt.

"Let's go, Kevin."

They found Manny and Tiger at the hospital, swollen and stitched. Manny was asleep, but Tiger, a youngster Helen guessed to be about fourteen, was awake and able to talk somewhat through his split lips.

"Who did this?"

"Outfit."

"You sure about that?" Kevin asked. "You've got to be positive."

Tiger nodded. "I knew some of them from when I first got to town. They're with Capone and Torrio now. I'm sure."

"Shit!" Helen spat. "We'll get to the bottom of this. But Kevin's right. You'd better be damned certain."

Tiger squeezed his eyes shut then, and Helen realized what an effort it was for him to talk.

"We're going to square up your bills then get to the bottom of this. Take a few days, kiddo."

Kevin stayed back as Helen paid the bill.

"What now, boss?" Kevin asked as them climbed back in the car.

"Gattino's."

"Someday Moretti might forget you guys used to work together on the street. He might get tired of you always hitting him up for information."

"Too bad. I need to know what happened out there today. I owe it to those kids."

They walked into Gattino's and strode back to Moretti's table.

"What happened today?" Helen asked.

"I don't know what you're talking about."

Helen glanced over at Maria, who quickly looked away.

"Someone messed up a couple of my guys, and I want to know why."

"Chicago's a dangerous city," Moretti said.

"Save it," she said, but her feeling of unease about Maria was starting to eat at her more than her kids getting jumped. Something about that dame really got under her skin.

"Look, I don't know everything that happens, you know? So maybe something went down that wasn't my Outfit."

"It was the Outfit all right." Helen didn't take her focus from Maria. "One of the guys recognized them."

"It wasn't my crew, though. Look, sometimes the boys get restless and like to take out aggressions. I can't stop that. Boys will be boys."

"Well, tell them to find someone else to jump next time. Or else."

"Or else what?"

"Just or else."

Helen pulled up a chair and sat next to Maria.

"What gives, doll? We've always had a good time, and now you act like you can't stand the sight of me. What's going on?"

"Why do you want to bother with me? Leave me be. Take care of your business and get out of here."

"Maybe I don't want to. Maybe I want to talk to you."

"I've got nothing to say to you."

"I wish you'd tell me what's eating you."

"Nothing."

"Maybe that's the problem." Helen stood and turned to Moretti. "Tell your goons to leave my guys alone. They weren't in your area."

"Says you. This whole town is our area. Don't you forget that."

Helen and Kevin drove to the Beaver to wind down.

"What's with that Maria?" Kevin asked.

"You noticed it, too?"

"What I noticed was you can't leave her alone. You're really trying to piss Moretti off, aren't you?"

"Have you looked at her? I mean, really looked at her? She's gorgeous."

"She's Moretti's. Capone's right-hand man's. You need to get her out of your head."

"I suppose I should. Maybe I'll go upstairs in a bit to get my mind off her."

"That's a good idea."

They had a few drinks and relaxed. It was a couple of hours later when Kevin said, "Oh shit. This can't be good."

Helen followed his gaze and found Maria once again at their bar.

"Check the perimeter," Helen said before walking up to the bar to see what was going on.

"Welcome back. To what do we owe this pleasure?"

"Can't a girl get a drink?"

"Sure. Why here? Why now?"

"Maybe I thought I was rude to you. Maybe I wanted to come say hello," Maria said.

"Her drinks are on me," Helen told the bartender, then put her hand on Maria's elbow and guided her to her table.

"I'm glad you're here, Maria. You sure this isn't a double-cross or anything?"

"It's not. I just felt bad. Franco and me got in another fight, and I just wanted to see you."

"Yeah?" Helen felt her heart flutter. Dare she dream she might have a chance with Maria yet? "Well, let's dance and forget about life for a while."

After a few songs, they sat back down.

"You really are swell to be around," Maria said.

"I'm glad, because I really like you."

"Franco says you're trouble," Maria said.

"Franco doesn't like a woman running her own gang."

"Franco thinks women are for fucking only."

Helen was immediately taken aback at Maria's vulgarity, but then laughed.

"I guess he would."

"Is there somewhere we can go talk?" Maria asked.

Helen's heart skipped a beat. "Sure. We can go to my office." She turned to Kevin. "Keep an eye on things."

She ignored the pointed look Kevin gave her and quickly escorted Maria past the bar and into her private office.

"Have a seat. I'll pour you a drink."

Helen's office was bigger than the rooms the girls upstairs used. It had a full bar along one wall, a leather couch along the other, and two loveseats. End tables by the couch had bronze table lamps with petal shades. It was masculine but comfortable, and Helen was happy to share it with Maria.

Maria sat on the couch and gratefully took her wine. Helen sat next to her.

"What did you want to talk about, doll?"

"I just wanted to get away from the crowds. It gets tiresome. You know, always being around a lot of people. Sometimes I like to be in a quiet place where I can hear myself think."

"That makes sense."

"It does? You feel that way? 'Cause Franco always has to be in the middle of some going on or other."

"I cherish my quiet time."

They sat in silence for a minute.

"I'm a little confused, doll. One minute you're giving me the bum's rush and the next you're at my bar in my office with me. What gives?"

"I'm sorry," Maria said.

Helen waited. When Maria said nothing else, Helen prodded. "You can see why I'm confused, though, right? Next time I see you, how will you be?"

"I'll try to be nice. I guess I got scared."

"Scared. Why? Have I ever been anything but nice to you?"

"Maybe you're too nice."

"What does that mean?" Helen asked.

"You always make me feel like I'm someone special when I'm around you."

Helen's stomach flip-flopped. She wanted to tell Maria what a delicate flower she thought she was and how special she deserved to be treated.

"So maybe I liked it too much," Maria continued.

"You should always feel special. Moretti don't deserve a gal like you."

"See? You're doing it again."

"Should I be sorry? Because I'm not. And I won't apologize for telling it like it is."

Maria reached out and cradled Helen's jaw. Helen saw a longing in the brown pools of Maria's eyes. She licked her lips, uncertain of what to do. As Maria caressed Helen's cheek, Helen bent forward. Her mind told her to stop, but her body urged her onward.

The banging on the door brought her to her senses.

"What gives?" she called.

"Moretti's boys are here. They're looking for Maria," Kevin answered.

Helen stood. "How did they know you were here?"

"I don't know. I didn't tell anyone."

"Well, someone knew, damn it." She placed their drinks on the bar and opened the door.

"Sorry, boss," Kevin said.

Maria stopped in the doorway. She kissed Helen's cheek before rushing out to greet the men.

"You may have really fucked up this time," Kevin said.

"Why? I didn't bring her here."

"Not to the bar. But you took her to your office."

"Nothing happened," Helen was happy to say honestly.

"You two sure looked guilty as hell."

"That's your dirty mind, Kevin. I'm telling you nothing happened. We talked is all."

"Well, I hope talking is all Moretti does to her."

"You said it, Kevin. You said it."

Chapter Seven

The phone in the hideout rang and Helen got up from the poker game to answer, assuming it was one of her men. It was one of the barbers.

"What's up, Brian?"

"There's some lady here. Says she knows you."

Helen's heart skipped. What woman would know to find her at the barbershop?

"Who is she?"

"Says her name's Maria and she needs to talk to you."

"I'll be right up."

Helen hurried to the barbershop, hoping Maria was okay. She found her shaken, not at all her usual sassy self.

"What are you doing here?" Helen asked.

"I needed to see you."

"So I hear. Come on. Let's get a cup of coffee."

She steered her out of the shop and down the street. They walked into a small coffee shop and Helen signaled to the owner for two cups. She sat with Maria at her usual table in the far back.

"What's going on?"

"Franco was really mad I went to the Beaver by myself," Maria said.

"And you think he's going to be happy you came here?"

"No. He thinks I'm going to double-cross him."

"You'd never do that."

"See? You understand me. He doesn't."

"So what gives, doll? Why would you take a chance and come over here?"

"I had to see you again."

Helen shook her head, her mind a jumble of racing thoughts. She was thrilled Maria wanted to see her again, but scared for her. She didn't want Maria in trouble with Moretti. She knew Franco had a temper.

"Sometimes a girl needs to be with other girls, you know?" Maria said.

"Surely there are Outfit molls you can do things with," Helen suggested, unsure of how to proceed. Part of her wanted to tell Maria to ditch Moretti and be hers, but if Maria was only looking for friendship, she had to tread lightly.

"They're not the same. All's they talk about is the latest dance moves or their makeup. You're different."

"I run my own outfit, so sure I'm not a moll. But Franco'd probably be happier if you stayed with them."

"So you don't want to see me?" Maria extended her lower lip, and Helen's crotch clenched. She longed to take that lip between hers.

"I just don't want you getting in trouble."

"You afraid?" The old, spitfire Maria was back.

Helen threw her head back and laughed.

"I'm not afraid of nothin'."

"Then let's go do something."

Helen hesitated only a moment. "Sure, doll. Let's catch a show."

"Really?"

"Sure. I've been wanting to see Charlie Chaplin's latest. Let's go find a matinee."

"That would be swell," Maria said.

Helen threw some coins on the table and guided Maria down the street to her car.

"So what does Franco think you're doing today?"

"He thinks I'm shopping. He won't care. As long as I'm ready to go to Gattino's at five, he'll be fine."

Helen drove to her favorite theater and paid for herself and Maria. They settled into their seats and watched the movie. Helen was beside herself to have this time with Maria. It was almost like a date, something she hadn't been on in years. She tried to relax and enjoy the movie, but was completely focused on Maria beside her. When Maria reached out and took her hand, she was aroused and confused. Maria clearly didn't know that she was playing with fire. Or did she?

The movie ended and Helen was sad to feel the weight of Maria's hand leave hers. They drove in silence back to the barbershop, where Helen hailed a cab for Maria.

"When will I see you again?" Maria asked.

"I don't know. You need to be careful with Franco."

"Okay. Well, thanks for today. That was fun."

"Sure thing. We'll do it again some time."

Maria slipped a piece of paper into Helen's pocket as she climbed in the cab. Helen waited until it was out of sight to find out what the paper was. It was Maria's phone number. She couldn't get the smile off her face as she walked around back to headquarters.

"Where you been, boss?" Kevin asked. "You left in a hurry."

"I had a friend stop by. We spent the afternoon together."

"Anyone we know?" he asked.

"Nobody important." Helen lied. "Let's go to the bar."

❖

March arrived and the new speakeasy was close to being finished.

"You guys been spreading the word about Lucky's opening on the seventeenth?" Helen asked her lieutenants.

"We're expecting quite a crowd," Marty said.

"That's what I want to hear. I want green beer and Irish music. I want it to be a Saint Patrick's Day party the likes of which Chicago has never seen. Are the girls all set to work?"

"We've got ten new gals who'll be upstairs. You're going to like them, boss."

"I'm sure I will. But remember, that first night they're for the customers only."

"Yeah, we know."

"Kevin, did you get the marijuana and the hashish lined up?"

"We're all set, boss. It's going to be a smash."

"Excellent. Well, let's go to the Beaver and have a few while it's still our only watering hole."

Helen strode into the bar with one hand in her pocket. She rubbed the paper between her thumb and finger. She had the number memorized, even though she'd never called it. Still, she kept it with her, telling herself she'd throw it away tomorrow. Always tomorrow.

She hadn't seen Maria since the movies, which she knew was her fault. The next move was hers, but she'd been so busy. She hoped Maria hadn't given up on her. She reasoned she'd probably been busy with Moretti anyway. Johnny Torrio had been arrested, so Al Capone was solely in charge of the Outfit. As Al's right-hand man, Moretti had to have taken on more responsibilities of late.

The bar was fun and the guys were all getting loose when Moretti, Maria, and some of his men walked in. Helen's men were immediately on alert, and Helen stiffened at the sight of Maria on Moretti's arm. She wanted her for her own.

"To what do we owe this visit?" she asked coolly when they reached her table.

"Word spreads fast in this town," Moretti said, sitting next to Helen. Maria sat on the other side of him, and Helen wished they'd switch seats. She wanted to sit next to her.

"Yeah? What are you hearing?"

"I'm hearing you're opening a new place."

"Free enterprise."

"You're just asking for trouble," Moretti said.

"How do you figure? It's one more gin joint in town. We're not hurting you."

"You'd better not. We'll be keeping an eye on it. Just know that."

"Don't you have enough to keep you busy?" Helen asked.

"I stay busy watching the competition."

"Well, then maybe you had better keep a closer eye on me." She stood and walked over to Maria. "Shall we dance?"

She smiled as Moretti struggled to maintain his composure while Maria stood and took Helen's hand.

"How come you haven't called?" Maria asked.

"Sorry, doll. I've been really busy."

"Sounds like it," Maria pouted.

"I've been thinking about you a lot, though," Helen said.

"Yeah? That's nice to hear. I think about you all the time. Can we go to another movie sometime maybe?"

"You're really trying to piss ol' Franco off, aren't you?"

"No. He's just so boring compared to you."

Helen beamed at the compliment. "I promise I'll call you and we'll do something. But I'm not sure how."

"Maybe I can go to the opening of your new speakeasy."

"That would really get under his skin."

"You're right. I don't care, though. I'm getting tired of him."

"Well, still, to keep the peace, we'll do things during the day. Maybe go to lunch tomorrow?"

"That'd be swell."

"Okay then. It's a date. Where shall I pick you up?"

Maria told Helen her address.

"You sure it's safe for me to go there? I bet Franco has your place watched."

"Don't be silly. You'll be fine. Just honk when you get there and I'll come down. I'll be waiting for you. You won't even have to get out of the car."

"That doesn't sound very chivalrous," Helen said.

"No, but it's safe. So tomorrow at one?"

"Tomorrow at one."

They danced a little more then walked back to the table. Moretti stood immediately.

"Where's the fire?" Helen asked.

"I've got better things to do than sit around here. You just be careful, Byrne."

"Will do." She bent to kiss Maria's knuckles and watched the curves of her hips as she walked out the door.

"Shit, boss. You're still stuck on Maria? You're going to get in a lot of trouble."

"What? Moretti doesn't deserve her."

"Well, you deserve better."

Helen shot him a look. "Watch your mouth, Kevin."

"Damn, kid, you've got it bad."

Chapter Eight

The next day at precisely one o'clock, Helen tooted her horn outside of Maria's room. She lived in a boarding house in the southern part of town. Helen couldn't wait to see her, but was anxious to get out of the neighborhood to safety.

Maria came downstairs in a navy blue sailor's dress that accented her dark skin. She wore a matching hat that all but covered her eyes. Helen thought she'd never looked better.

"You look swell," she said when Maria slid in the car.

"Thanks. I'm glad you like it. Where are you taking me?"

"I'm taking you to a little place on the West Side."

"Well, I expected that." Maria laughed, a sound that filled Helen with warmth.

They pulled up in front of a Cuban restaurant that Helen's gang provided protection for. She knew they'd be safe there.

She opened Maria's door and took her hand as she helped her out. Maria did not let go as they walked into the restaurant. Helen held tight to the soft hand in hers as she approached the maître d'.

"Is my usual table available?"

"Of course, Miss Byrne. Right this way."

He led them to a table in the back of the restaurant with a wonderful view of the garden it was built around.

"This place is real pretty," Maria said.

"Thanks. It's a favorite of mine."

"I'm glad you weren't too busy today. I've really missed you."

"I've missed you, too, doll."

"I thought you'd forgotten about me."

"Not a chance."

"Tell me about this new speakeasy," Maria said in a low voice.

"Franco should know all about it."

"But I want to know."

Helen wondered briefly if Moretti was trying to set her up. As much as she hoped not, she opted on the side of caution.

"Let's not talk about work."

"Fine," Maria said. "Tell me about young Helen Byrne. What were you like as a child?"

"I think I'd rather talk about work."

Lunch passed quickly, too quickly for Helen. She wanted to spend more time with Maria.

"I'd like to see you again," she said as she pulled up in front of Maria's apartments.

"I'd like that. Call me." Maria kissed her on the cheek.

Helen fought the urge to pull her to her and kiss her on the lips. She wanted Maria so desperately.

"You sure you know what you want?" Helen asked.

"I think I do." Maria winked and let herself out of the car.

❖

Helen was dressed in a black suit with a Kelly green shirt and a green carnation boutonniere. She knew she looked good and felt good as she strolled into Lucky's with Kevin for its grand opening. The place was jumpin' and Helen felt a sense of pride at all the hard work her men had done to get it ready and open.

She recognized many of the patrons from the Golden Beaver, but was pleased to see a lot of new faces. She assumed they were from the neighborhood, and she liked that her gang had been welcomed. She knew they'd been receiving protection money from most of the businesses, but that didn't always mean they were liked. The showing at Lucky's said something, to be sure.

Helen grabbed one of the working girls and led her to the dance floor. They danced a set before a beefy gentleman cut in and took the girl from her. Helen smiled to herself as she left the floor, thinking of the money the girls upstairs would be making that night.

The evening passed gaily, with green beer and liquor flowing. Helen was nursing her drink at her table when Moretti and Maria walked in surrounded by large men.

She crossed the bar to meet them, rather than wait at her table.

"We don't want any trouble, Franco. Tell your goons to stand down."

"They're not here for trouble," Moretti said. "They're just here to check things out. Same as us."

"Come on back to my table then." Helen took Maria's hand, and Moretti and his men followed.

"Did you hear about the crossfire today?" Moretti asked when they were seated.

Helen was immediately attentive. "What crossfire was that?"

"Some guys from Weiss's outfit got in a shootout with some of the boys from the Eastside. Some civilians got killed in the crossfire. The heat has been significantly turned up."

"That's not good. But why are you telling me this?"

"Just making conversation."

"If you're trying to scare me, it ain't working."

"Not trying to scare you. Just keeping you informed. Thought you might find it interesting."

"I'm not interested in going after either gang, Franco. I'm keeping to myself these days. Or hadn't you noticed?"

"You opened a new speakeasy, just blocks from our territory. That ain't laying low."

"It's not in your territory," Helen said. "And we're not taking business away from you."

"Says you. And maybe not right now, but it's only the first night. If you do start taking business away, there's going to be trouble."

"I'm not worried. You have enough businesses already."

"You know Big Al as well as I do. There's no such thing as enough businesses." He smiled.

"Come on, Maria," Helen stood and offered her hand. "Let's dance."

They danced the quick steps to the music for several songs before the band slowed the tempo. Maria moved into Helen's arms.

"I like being close to you," Maria said softly.

"It's nice," Helen said.

"Are you going to show me your office here?"

"Not while Franco's here."

"Aw," Maria pouted. "Why not?"

Helene's crotch spasmed at the sight of the protruding lower lip. She ached to take it between her lips and suck on it. She swallowed hard.

"Don't do that," she growled.

"Do what?"

"Never mind."

The song ended and Helen escorted her back to the table.

"Nice place you've got here, Byrne," Moretti said.

"Thanks. We like it."

"Show me around?" Maria asked.

Helen looked over at Moretti, who nodded slightly.

"Sure. Why not?" She stood and pulled Maria's chair out for her. When they were out of earshot of the table, she said, "You sure like to get what you want, don't you?"

"You know it." She smiled.

"You really just want to see my office, don't you?"

"Yes."

"Why?"

"Because I like the strength and masculinity of your office at the other place. I like the feel of it. It feels like you so I want to see this one, too."

Helen was unsure about showing off her inner sanctum to Big Al's best man's best girl. But the idea of being alone in a room with Maria completely out of sight of prying eyes was too much. She opened a door that looked like it would hold a closet and guided Maria up a back staircase.

"Isn't upstairs where the prostitutes work?" Maria asked.

"You know your way around a speakeasy, don't you?"

"I pay attention."

"I bet you do."

They passed several doors before Helen stopped and opened one. She stood back and let Maria enter first. She walked in after her and was filled with pride as she looked at the leather sofa and matching wing chairs, the mahogany bar, and the pictures of Chicago on the wall.

"This is really nice, Helen," Maria said.

The sound of her name on Maria's lips made her heart swell. She slipped her hands in her pockets and stepped away from Maria, hoping some distance would ease the dizziness she was feeling.

"You like me, don't you?" Maria asked, moving near Helen again.

"Of course I do, doll. Why?"

"Sometimes I wonder."

"Sure I do. I think you're swell."

Maria leaned into Helen.

"It just seems to me that if you liked me enough you'd kiss me."

Helen tried to formulate a reasonable argument, but couldn't. She said lamely, "But you're Franco's girl."

"But I could be yours." She snaked her arms around Helen.

Helen licked her lips, which were suddenly bone dry. Her stomach was in knots, her want wrestling with her logic. She could cause a big brouhaha if she took Moretti's girl. But isn't that what she wanted? Hadn't she wanted Maria for a long time? Still, she'd never dared to dream it could actually become a reality.

"Don't you want me, Helen?" Maria cooed.

Helen moved her arms around Maria and held her close. She reveled in the feel of their bodies pressed together. She lowered her mouth to lightly kiss Maria's neck, her heart rate soaring at the feel of the warm skin and the heady scent of her perfume.

She kissed Maria's cheek, then moved her hand to cup her jaw, her thumb lightly tracing it. She looked into Maria's eyes and saw a desire that matched her own. She ran her thumb over Maria's parted lips and heard her sharp intake of breath. She knew once she kissed her, there would be no turning back. And she knew she was going to kiss her. She had to.

Helen saw Maria's eyes close as she bent toward her. She closed her eyes and felt the softness of Maria's lips under hers. Her body was alive; tension soared through every inch of her as she tried to rise up. Maria pulled her back and opened her mouth, offering Helen entry. Helen moved her tongue into the moist heat of Maria's mouth, dancing with Maria's tongue. Her pants were drenched. She pulled Maria tighter, craving more of her.

When the kiss finally ended, it took Helen a minute to find her voice.

"I should get you back downstairs."

"But I want to stay here with you."

Helen didn't say anything.

"So what now?" Maria asked.

"What do you mean?"

"I could go tell Franco to get lost right now and stay with you."

"Now's not the time. He'd never forgive us. We'll play it by ear. Just act like nothing's going on for now. Then you can leave him."

"I want to stay here with you, Helen. I mean, for the night. Wouldn't that be nice?"

The blood rushed in Helen's ears as thoughts and desires coursed through her.

"Yes, that would be nice. It would be better than nice." She laughed. "But not tonight. Not yet."

"When?"

"I don't know. Just not now. Now come on. Let me get you back downstairs."

Helen felt like she had guilt written all over her face as she approached the table. She wanted to smile ear to ear, but fought to keep her face straight.

"You happy now?" Moretti asked Maria.

"I am."

"You've got the lay of the land? I swear I should use you as one of the guys." He laughed and Helen joined him, hoping her laughter sounded natural and not nervous.

"Yep, she knows this place inside out now," Helen said.

Franco stood. "We're leaving now. But remember that we're keeping an eye on you. We won't have you getting too big."

"I'm small-time, Franco," Helen said.

"Still, we won't settle for you taking what's ours."

Helen blanched, knowing that's exactly what she was doing with Maria.

Maria gave Helen a meaningful look as she took Moretti's arm and allowed him to escort her out.

Chapter Nine

"They killed Frank Capone yesterday," Kevin told Helen when she arrived at headquarters an early April morning.

"Who did?"

"The cops."

"No shit?"

"Yep. It happened at the polls."

"Al's gonna be looking for blood now," Helen said.

"At least they won't be looking at us for a while."

"True." Helen thought quickly of Maria. She'd be able to see her easily now while the gang had its attention elsewhere.

"Where'd you go, boss?"

"What do you mean?"

"You just went a million miles away right there. What are you thinking about? Are we gonna make a move now?"

"No. While Capone's focus will be on revenge, he's going to want blood no matter where it comes from. No reason for it to be ours he spills."

"Good point."

Helen managed to stay focused as the rest of her lieutenants arrived with their weekly takes. She locked up the bulk of it in the safe and gave the men their share to split among their teams. The men broke out cards and started a game of poker, which Helen declined to join. She excused herself and left the building.

She hurried to her apartment up the street and called Maria.

"Hello?" The voice on the other end of the line sounded like heaven.

"Hey, doll. How you doin?"

"Hey yourself!" Maria sounded excited. "How've you been? I've missed you."

"I've missed you, too. I want to see you."

"When?"

"Now. Can I pick you up for lunch?"

"Sure. I can be ready in a half hour."

Helen was at the boarding house precisely thirty minutes later. Her heart skipped a beat when she saw Maria walking down the front stairs. She wanted her more than ever. She held the door open for her and admired her shapely legs as Maria slid into the car.

"Where are we going?" Maria asked.

"I figured we'd grab a bite then head back to my place to talk."

They ate a leisurely lunch at a small café a few blocks from Lucky's. Afterward, Helen drove them to a penthouse she had recently rented nearby. They took the elevator to the top floor.

"What a beautiful view," Maria said.

Helen sidled up behind her, wrapped her arms around her, and kissed her neck.

"You sure smell good."

Maria leaned back into her. She closed her hands over Helen's.

Helen turned her around to face her. She closed her mouth over Maria's and tasted her sweetness.

"I'm ready to leave Franco for you," Maria said. "Just say when."

"Shhh. No talking." Helen kissed her again, this time prying her lips apart with her tongue. Maria opened her mouth, and Helen reveled in the feel of their tongues playing together.

Helen was breathless when the kiss ended.

"I need you," she whispered hoarsely.

"Take me."

Helen took Maria to her room and kissed her again, passionately and possessively. She unbuttoned Maria's dress. She slid it to the floor and stepped back, admiring the sensual body.

"You're beautiful, Maria."

Maria unhooked her bra and let it fall to the floor, allowing Helen to gaze upon her pert breasts, her nipples taut with need.

Helen's breath caught at the sight. She lovingly cupped one breast in her hand, running her thumb over the nipple. She watched as Maria's eyes closed in pleasure.

She kissed Maria's neck as she slid her slip over her shapely hips and down to join the bra and dress on the floor.

Maria was naked, save for her panties. Helen wanted to peel them off with her teeth, but determined to make herself wait. She bent and took a nipple in her mouth, licking it slowly and tugging gently. She felt Maria's hands in her hair and was encouraged to pull more deeply on the treasure in her mouth.

"You make me feel so good," Maria whispered.

"You haven't felt anything yet."

Helen moved to the other nipple and sucked on it intently, losing herself in the action. She breathed the scent of Maria's skin, felt her heat against her. She knew she was right where she belonged.

Helen stepped back from Maria and gently laid her on the bed. She quickly undressed, never taking her gaze off Maria. She noted Maria's appreciative stare and felt her body flush with desire.

When she lay next to Maria, Maria moved to slide her panties off.

"Not yet," Helen said.

"But you're naked."

"Yes. And you will be soon."

Helen knew she was teasing them both mercilessly but couldn't resist. When she was ready to lay Maria bare, it would be an amazing moment. She wanted to draw it out.

She kissed Maria again, her hand skimming over her curves. Her skin was so soft, yet it prickled at Helen's touch. Soon, she was covered in gooseflesh, most prominently her areolas.

Helen licked and sucked first one nipple, then the other as she ran her hand between her legs to caress the wet crotch of her panties. She pressed it into her, feeling her swollen clit beneath it. She moved the panties to the side and let her fingers tease the soft area underneath.

"You're making me crazy," Maria moaned.

"Just relax and enjoy it."

"Oh, I'm enjoying it all right."

Helen kissed Maria's mouth again then peeled her soaked panties down her legs. She kissed down Maria's body until she was kneeling between her legs. She eased her knees apart and drew a deep breath, savoring the heady smell of Maria.

She leaned her cheek against Maria's soft inner thigh and admired the sight before her. When she could wait no more, she circled Maria's clit with her tongue. Her flavor was rich and delicious, just as she'd known it would be. She moved her tongue lower and tasted all of her, dipping her tongue inside and lapping away, savoring the flavor.

Helen moved her hand up Maria's body and closed on her breast, which she kneaded and squeezed before pinching her nipple.

Maria moved against Helen, pressing herself against her as much as she could. Helen loved how responsive she was. She was a natural to please. She heard Maria's breathing growing more and more shallow. She felt her hand on her head, pressing her to her center. She licked and sucked fervently until Maria cried out, frozen against her as the orgasm washed over her.

When she finally relaxed, Helen started anew, quickly taking Maria to the edge again and again.

Helen climbed next to Maria and took her in her arms.

"You were amazing, baby," Maria whispered.

"So were you, doll."

Maria rolled over and ran her hands over Helen's chest.

"I want to make you feel like that."

"You will, doll. You'll learn to. For now, just relax and let me hold you."

❖

Helen dropped Maria off and headed for the office, a spring in her step. She found the men getting ready to go to Lucky's.

"I'll join you," she said.

"I'll drive you, boss," Kevin said.

When they were in his car, he cast her a sidelong glance.

"You sure are in a good mood. What have you been doing today?"

"Nothing in particular."

"Why don't I buy that? You're up to something. Spill."

"So maybe I spent the afternoon with a special lady."

"That's good to hear," Kevin said. "I'd like to see you get your mind off that Maria gal."

When Helen didn't say anything, Kevin slammed on the brakes.

"You weren't with Maria, were you?"

"Maybe I was. So what?"

Kevin continued driving. "You're gonna get in a lot of trouble, Helen."

"No, I'm not. We're discreet and no one will find out."

"I'm worried."

"Don't be."

Lucky's was jumping that evening. Helen didn't recognize a lot of people, which was a good sign. New people meant word of mouth was spreading. That was always good for business.

The gang sat at a big table in the back and watched the dancers and the celebrants. She noted several men approaching the working girls and disappearing up the stairs. She smiled. Life was good.

It was getting late and Helen was saying her good-byes. Kevin asked if he could see her in the office, so they retreated up the back staircase.

"What's up?" she asked.

"I can't stop thinking about Maria," Kevin said.

"Really? Let it go. I'm a big girl."

"But there's a lot at stake here. Moretti's not gonna take you stealing his best girl lying down."

"Come on. Those guys treat their girls like a dime a dozen. They won't care."

Before Kevin could answer, they heard the rat-a-tat of gunfire downstairs followed by screaming. Kevin threw Helen on the floor and covered her until they heard the sounds of squealing tires.

"You okay?" he asked, helping her up.

"I'm fine. I appreciate you covering me, but I wasn't in danger."

"You never know."

"Let's get down there and see the damage."

They found bloodied bodies all around and saw the booze bottles all shot up. There were bullet holes in several of the walls. Helen's men were immediately around her.

"You guys get the wounded out of here and to hospitals," she said to them.

"Kevin, call Flander's and get them here to pick up the dead. Shit. Who did this?"

"Moretti's men," one of her lieutenants said.

"Are you sure?"

"Positive."

Kevin gave Helen a warning look before he left to make his call.

"Shit," Helen repeated.

Chapter Ten

"What are we gonna do about Moretti?" Kevin asked the next day at their headquarters.

"We need to send a message back to him, for sure," one of the men said.

Kevin looked at Helen. "What do you say?"

"First priority is to get Lucky's back open for business," she said. "Where are we on that?"

"We're moving booze from the Beaver over and we have more on its way."

"Good. I want to know when Capone is supposed to get his next shipment. We'll help ourselves to some."

"I'll see what I can find out," one of her men said, picking up the phone.

"In the meantime, you guys get your men together and get back here. We're going to retaliate soon, and I want it to be organized."

Her lieutenants returned within an hour and the office was filled with men hungry for blood. They sat quietly, trained on Helen, awaiting orders.

"I want to hurt Capone in his wallet," Helen said. "Tomorrow night, I want you to hit his gambling joint over by the Hawthorne Hotel. You know the one Moretti runs. Be sly and quiet in your approach, then shoot the place up like they did us. You'll have to be careful, though, because they'll be vigilant."

"Moretti's having a big tournament in three weeks," Kevin said. "Can we wait that long?"

"Sure we can wait. They'll have dropped their guard by then. Good idea, Kevin."

She turned and faced the younger men on the other side of the room.

"You guys get out there and hit the boys at the newspapers. Stick with Moretti's territory. I don't want anyone thinking they're safe from us. The rest of you get out there and make your presence known. Don't give anyone any reason to think we're scared or backing down."

They all nodded their understanding and Helen dismissed them.

"And you?" Kevin asked.

"What about me?"

"What are you going to do about your situation?"

"My situation isn't changing." Helen was frustrated as she left the building.

She drove to Maria's place and knocked on the door. An older woman answered and Helen asked for Maria. She was invited in and waited in a well-appointed sitting room. The winged back chairs were worn, but the doilies on their arms attempted to cover the faded cloth. The small round table had a vase of flowers that were obviously due to be changed. Somehow Helen had imagined the place Maria lived to be nicer. She was depressed by her surroundings.

Her mood improved the minute Maria walked into the room. She looked beautiful in a red dress cut low enough to tease Helen with what lay beneath.

"Did you hear about last night?" Helen asked.

"I did. I'm so sorry."

"Does Franco know about us?"

"I haven't said anything to him."

"He must be having you watched," Helen said.

"I don't think I'm that important to him."

"Will you be with him tonight?"

"I'd rather be with you," Maria said.

"I'd rather you be with me, too. But I think you should stick with him a little while longer."

"I hate that. It's so hard. And it's not the same. He's not as exciting or as caring as you are."

"I appreciate that," Helen said. "But unless we want a lot of people dying, we need to play it cool."

"Not too cool, I hope." Maria took Helen's hand and led her to her room. She kissed her as soon as the door closed behind them.

Helen's head spun at the intensity of the kiss. She pulled Maria tight and kissed her again, letting her hands run up and down her body.

Maria unbuttoned Helen's shirt and slid her hands inside. She caressed Helen through her undershirt.

Helen stepped back. "Are you sure this is a good place for this?"

"Why not?" She stepped over and locked the door then took Helen in her arms again.

As they kissed, Maria slipped her hands under the undershirt and rubbed her hands over Helen's breasts.

Helen kissed Maria's neck and chest, fighting to concentrate over the sensations she was feeling. She groaned when Maria closed her fingers on her nipples.

"Doll, you're making me crazy."

"Good." She stepped back and took Helen's shirt and undershirt off. She unbuttoned and unzipped her pants and backed up so Helen could step out of them.

Helen undressed Maria and they fell into bed. Maria climbed on top of Helen, straddling her middle. She rubbed on her while she sucked her nipples. Helen rested her hands on Maria's hips, guiding her as she ground into her.

Maria moved lower on Helen, finally settling between her legs.

"I want to please you like you please me."

"No pressure, doll. Just do what comes naturally."

Helen felt Maria's tongue just under her clit. Maria teased her before tasting inside her. Helen gripped the sheet, feeling herself spiral as Maria worked her. Her tongue was deep, and Helen felt like she was licking her very soul. She closed her eyes and lost herself in the feelings. She arched her back, pressing herself into Maria. Helen was amazed at how skilled Maria was. She'd never been with a woman, but she was making Helen feel things she'd never felt before.

Helen tried to make herself hold out, but Maria was too insistent. She pressed Maria's face into her as she rode her tongue to a powerful climax.

"Shit, doll. That was amazing!"

"I'm so glad you liked it."

"Let me show you how much."

Helen sucked on Maria's nipples while she slipped her hand between her legs, finding her wet and ready for her. She traced the whole area before dragging her fingers around her clit, teasing Maria by not touching it directly.

"Please, baby," Maria mewed.

Helen buried her fingers inside her, stroking her as she continued to suckle.

"Oh my God, you feel good." Maria moved her hips in time with Helen.

Helen pressed hard against her as she withdrew her fingers and moved them to Maria's swollen clit. She rubbed it hard and fast until Maria cried out as she came.

Maria curled up against Helen, lazily drawing circles on her chest.

"You're amazing," she said.

"You're pretty amazing yourself," Helen said. "You sure I'm your first woman?"

"I'm sure." Maria laughed.

"Well, you're a natural."

"I just did what felt right."

"And you did it so well," Helen said.

They lay quietly until Helen knew she had to get to work.

"Hey, doll, I need to get going."

"Aw. Do you have to?"

"I do." She kissed Maria's forehead. "I'm sorry, but I've got work to do."

"When will I see you again?"

"Soon, I hope."

"I hope so, too."

❖

Helen arrived at headquarters to find Kevin pacing, while the others played cards and smoked cigars.

"What's got you upset, Kevin?"

"Where have you been?"

"Since when do I check in with you every moment of every day?" She poured herself a bourbon and water.

"Some of Moretti's men were seen casing the neighborhood by the Beaver," Kevin said.

"Who saw them?"

"Gus and Tommy were coming out of the Beaver. They saw them driving down the street. They was goin' really slow."

"Shit. I hope they leave us alone for a while. I want things to die down before our big hit."

"I think you're the only one that can make that happen," Kevin said.

"Give it a rest," Helen said. "Let's go to the Beaver. I don't want anyone thinking they can keep us away from there. You all go round up your men. I want a full crowd there tonight."

The place wasn't as jumping as Helen would have liked. Clearly, news of Lucky's had people scared. Still, there was a decent crowd and her men all seemed to be having a good time.

"Hey, baby." Katherine walked over to Helen. "I haven't seen you in a while. You up for a little fun?"

"Thanks, but I think I'll pass tonight. You go work the crowd."

She watched Katherine walk off and immediately be approached by a customer. Helen knew Katherine preferred women, but appreciated the good job she did for the business.

"You really are hooked on that Maria, aren't you?" Kevin whispered in her ear.

"I just want Katherine to make me some money. What's wrong with that?"

"I think you don't want to be with anyone but Moretti's girl."

"Do you have to call her that?" Helen asked.

"That's who she is, like it or not."

As if on cue, Moretti walked in with Maria following him. Helen cringed at the sight, but noted that at least she wasn't hanging on to his arm, anyway.

She watched her men as they eyed the two walk in surrounded by Moretti's goons. Every one of her men was trained on the group. Helen stayed seated while Kevin rose. She wouldn't give them an easy target, if that was their intention.

"What brings you here?" Kevin asked.

Moretti ignored him and pulled up two chairs so he and Maria could sit next to Helen.

"How was your day, Helen?" he asked.

"It was fine. Yours?"

"Not bad."

"What were your guys doin' cruising our turf?"

Moretti laughed and shook his head. "You really don't get it, do you? It's all our turf. We can cruise wherever we want."

"Look, we haven't done anything to you. You need to back the fuck off."

"Big words from such a small player."

Helen fumed. She didn't appreciate the way Moretti was talking to her. He had no right.

"If I'm so small then why won't your people leave me alone?"

"I think you know the answer to that. And you're not exactly laying low. Some of our boys got beaten up pretty bad today. I heard it was your order."

"Funny, some people got shot up in my place last night. I heard it was your order."

"Rumors," Moretti said.

Helen couldn't take it any longer. She needed to do something. She couldn't just sit there steaming at Moretti.

"Maria, you want to dance?" She stood and extended her hand.

"She don't want to dance with you," Moretti said.

Maria stood and took Helen's hand, glaring at Franco. Helen led her away from the table to the floor. They danced some fast numbers, but when the music slowed, Maria moved into Helen's arms.

"You're playing a dangerous game right now," Helen whispered in her ear.

"And you're not?"

"I shouldn't be holding you right under his nose."

"I don't see you letting go," Maria said.

"No, I'd be crazy to do that."

When the song ended, they walked back to the table. Helen was surprised that Moretti stayed seated. She'd fully expected him to storm out. She wondered what was going on under his calm, cool exterior.

"So when do you think you'll be able to open the other place again?" Moretti asked.

"Why are you asking?"

"Just making conversation."

"I bet."

"So?" he asked again. "When?"

"Any day now, thanks for asking."

When he didn't respond, she asked, "When are you planning on shooting up this place?"

"You're getting paranoid in your old age," he said.

"After last night, we see your guys staking out our neighborhood. That doesn't sound like paranoia to me."

"We own this town, Helen. You need to remember that. We'll go where we want when we want. And if you try to take what's ours, you'll pay."

He stood then, pulling Maria with him. His men closed ranks around him. Helen watched them walk off, his words echoing in her ears.

"I hope you were listening," Kevin said.

"I heard him."

"And?"

"And nothing."

"I'm glad you heard him. I just hope you listen to him."

"That clown can't tell me how to live my life. I didn't get where I am by worrying about what others thought I should and shouldn't do," Helen said.

"This is different, boss. You know that."

"I know nothing of the sort."

Chapter Eleven

Helen sat in headquarters looking over the books when Kevin burst through the door.

"Someone shot Maloney and Barton last night," he said.

"As in *Officers* Maloney and Barton?" Helen was shocked.

"The very same. Killed 'em both dead."

"Shit! How did it happen?"

"They were walking the beat over by Lucky's and someone drove by and shot them."

"Damn! They've been on our payroll almost as long as we have," she said. "Who got 'em?"

"Don't know. No one seems to have seen anything."

"Okay. Well, get the guys here. We're not taking this lying down."

"What are we gonna do?"

"Let me think. Just call the men."

"We can't go shooting cops, Helen. That would call too much attention to us."

"We need to make sure people know they can't shoot our men. That's all there is to it."

When the men had gathered, Helen told them her plan.

"I want you"—she pointed to the left side of the room—"to drive through Hymie's neighborhood up north. I want you to take out two of his men. I don't care who they are, but I want them dead."

She turned to the rest. "I want you to drive through the South and take out two of Capone's men. Again, it doesn't matter how high or low they are in the organization. I just want two dead. And don't anyone come back until it's done."

Kevin stayed behind with Helen.

"I hope you know what you're doing."

"We're not going to just sit back and let them take potshots at our people."

"But we don't know who did it. If it was Moretti again, we're rattling the cage of Hymie Weiss for no reason."

"But if it was Weiss's men, they need to know we're not going to let them get away with that."

"I just think we should have dug deeper to find out who did it before we retaliated."

"And that's why you're not the boss, Kevin. You can't be afraid in this business."

"I guess that is why you're the boss."

Kevin poured himself a cup of coffee and added booze from his flask.

"Liquid courage, Kevin?"

"You know it."

Helen poured herself a cup of coffee, but eschewed adding alcohol. She wanted to keep her wits about her. She continued going over the books, focusing on the amount she would have delivered to Maloney and Barton's widows. She took the money and put it in two separate envelopes and set them aside in the safe.

"I want you to take this to the widows. Not now, though. Give it some time. Next week, maybe."

"Will do, boss. Are we going to the funeral?"

"We are. We'll take some protection, but other than that, it'll just be you and me."

Several hours later, Helen was relieving Kevin of some of his hard earned money in poker. They set their cards down when the first group of men returned. They entered the room dragging a man named Marvin behind them.

"What happened?"

"They returned fire. Marvin was hit."

"Why isn't he at the hospital?" She looked at the man covered in blood with his head listing to one side.

"It wouldn't have done any good."

She felt his neck and realized he was gone.

"Lay him on the cot. Someone call Flander's. Shit."

The men from the South came in shortly after, having completed their mission without a hitch. They saw Marvin on the cot and fell quiet.

"What happened?"

"One of Hymie's men shot back."

The men from Flander's took Marvin away, and the room was silent. Helen had nothing to say to offer comfort. The only good thing was that it was the North and not Capone's men who did the deed. If it had been Capone's, her gang would have been more discouraged, or so she reasoned.

Helen told the men they'd done a good job and to take the rest of the day off. The men didn't leave, still shell-shocked from losing another man. Three men in twelve hours didn't help Helen's mood either. All she wanted was some comfort, and she only knew of one place to get it.

She pulled up in front of Maria's home and knocked on the door. Once again, she was shown in by the nice lady and waited in the same room she had before.

Maria came out of her room, took one look at Helen, and hugged her tight.

"What happened? You look horrible."

"It's been a rough day," Helen said. "Can we get out of here?"

"Sure. Let me get my purse."

They drove in silence to one of Helen's apartments, and Helen finally poured herself a stiff drink.

"Baby, what happened today?"

"We lost three men."

"I'm so sorry." She wrapped her arms around Helen again. "Do you want to talk about it?"

"No. I want to forget about it."

"Can you do that?" Maria seemed surprised.

"I can if you help me." She downed her drink, set the glass on the bar, then wrapped her arms around Maria.

"What can I do for you?" Maria asked.

Helen kissed her passionately, almost bruising her lips in her need. Maria opened her mouth to allow Helen access. They kissed until Helen was breathless. She rested her forehead against Maria's.

"I need you."

"I'm here for you."

Helen unbuttoned Maria's dress and gazed at her as the dress slid down her body and hit the floor. She reached around her and unhooked her bra, catching her breasts as the bra joined the dress.

"My God, you're beautiful," Helen whispered.

"I'm glad you think so." Maria stepped out of her panties and stood bare for Helen, who quickly stripped out of her own clothes. They stood skin to skin as they kissed again, this time long and slow.

Helen kissed and nipped at Maria's neck and sucked on her earlobe. She wanted all of her. She needed her to take her mind off the day. She pushed all thoughts of the policemen and Marvin out of her mind as she kissed Maria's mouth again.

She moved her hands to cover Maria's breasts and lightly squeezed them. She was rewarded with the feel of hard nipples poking her palms.

"Let's go lie down," Maria whispered against Helen's mouth.

They lay on the bed and Helen rolled on top of Maria, claiming her mouth. She kissed her hard, running her tongue around the inside of her mouth. She thought of nothing but pleasing the woman under her.

She kissed down her cheek to her neck, stopping to nibble where it met her shoulders. She kissed lower and took a hard nipple in her mouth. She rolled it on her tongue, sucking hard while Maria moaned loudly.

Helen slipped her hand between Maria's legs and quickly claimed her by entering her. She felt Maria closing around her and lost herself in the feelings of her satin walls she stroked. She plunged deeper with each thrust and Maria rose to meet her every time.

Maria wrapped her legs around Helen, opening herself to take her deeper. Helen moved her mouth to Maria's other nipple and sucked on it while she continued to move inside her. She slowed her movements and finally eased out of her, stroking her hardened clit.

"Oh, God, baby. You're making me crazy," Maria said.

Helen kissed down Maria's soft belly and ran her tongue over her clit while she moved her fingers back inside. Maria cried out as the force of the orgasm rolled over her.

Helen lay back, breathing heavily from the exertion of their lovemaking. She felt Maria's mouth on her own nipple and ran her hand through her hair. She watched as Maria sucked and pulled the nipple, her eyes closed.

She felt Maria's hand between her legs, exploring. Helen spread her legs wide, enjoying the tentative touches. Maria stroked her clit, over it and around it, feeling it swell at her touch.

"You sure make me feel good, doll."

"I'm glad. I want to make you feel like you make me feel." She moved her hand lower and slid her fingers inside Helen.

"Oh yeah. That's it," Helen whispered. She bucked against Maria, driving her deeper, faster.

Maria moved to take her hand out, but Helen quickly placed her hand on her wrist.

"No. Don't stop."

Maria continued until Helen could wait no longer. She allowed herself to crash through the wall and float into oblivion.

"Mm. I kind of like when you have a bad day," Maria said as she lay next to Helen.

Helen took her in her arms.

"That's not funny."

"I'm sorry. I can't imagine doing what you do, Helen. Honest."

"Thank you for that. It's not always easy. That's for sure."

"You're a good boss, though. I'm sure of that. I can tell from the hurt I saw in your eyes earlier."

"I really don't want to talk about it, Maria."

"Okay, baby. We won't. Why don't we talk about you taking me to dinner? I'm famished."

"That sounds good. Let's get dressed."

Helen took Maria out for dinner, then dropped her off at the boarding house before heading back to headquarters.

There were a few men still there. She noticed the cot was clean; all evidence of Marvin had been cleaned away.

"What's going on with you guys?" she asked.

"Nothing," Kevin said, slurring his words slightly.

"You men just been drinking all day?"

"You told us we were off duty," one of her lieutenants said.

"And you are. I wasn't judging. Just asking."

"I guess we all handle our grief differently." Kevin looked pointedly at her. "Where have you been?"

"Handling my grief."

"Lucky's reopened," one of her men said. "We should go check it out."

"Sounds good to me." She looked at Kevin. "I'll drive."

They arrived to find the speakeasy relatively quiet. A band was playing, and several people were dancing, but the patrons at the tables were few and far between. Still, Helen and her men got their drinks and sat at their table.

Several of the working girls came over and joined them. The men disappeared upstairs one at a time, and soon Kevin and Helen were left with a few of the women.

"You go on upstairs, boss," Kevin said. "I'll be okay down here."

"No. I'll stay here. Thanks."

The working girls scattered when the door opened and in walked Maria, Moretti, and his goons.

"Shit," Helen said.

"You can say that again," Kevin said.

Moretti sauntered over to Helen's table and sat down. At first, he sat quietly, simply looking around the club.

"Things are a little slow here," he said.

Helen shrugged. "We'll be busy again soon enough."

"Not if you don't think about what you're doing."

"What's that mean?" Helen asked.

"I heard you were behind the two men we lost today."

"I don't know anything about that. But maybe you can tell me about the two cops that were shot last night in this neighborhood?"

"I don't know what you're talking about."

"Says you."

"What cops, and why would you care?"

"They were friends," Helen said.

"I see."

Helen let her guard down slightly and allowed herself to revel in Maria's closeness. She swore she could feel the warmth radiating off her.

"You want to dance, doll?"

"I think she's fine where she is," Moretti said.

Maria stood. "I think I'd like to dance."

"Sit down," Moretti growled.

"Maybe you two should leave," Kevin said.

Moretti stood. "I think we will. You watch your step, Byrne. You're treading on thin ice right now."

"Tell your men to leave us alone," Helen said.

"You focus on what's yours," Moretti said. "Keep to yourself or there'll be trouble."

"He's an ass," Helen said as the entourage left.

"He is. But he's a powerful ass. And he don't like you messin' with his woman."

"We don't know he knows."

"Come on, boss. He knows."

Helen sipped her bourbon, remembering how beautiful Maria had looked. She just wanted to hold her every time she saw her. She had it bad, but Maria was so good. And she may be on Moretti's arm tonight, but she'd been in Helen's bed earlier. Helen was almost ready to have her leave Moretti for good. She didn't like sharing. Especially not with a goon like Franco Moretti.

Chapter Twelve

The rain fell on the small crowd that attended Marvin's funeral. He was young and had no family in the area. Helen searched her memory but couldn't recall ever hearing where Marvin was from. So there was no one to notify. She and Kevin and a few of Marvin's closest friends were in attendance. They watched as the casket was lowered into the ground.

Helen was tired of being a punching bag for the big gangs in the city. She vowed to get even with them for taking out her men. Of course, it was a gamble whenever she sent them on a hit that someone would return fire. It was part of the game they played. She needed to come up with another hit and soon.

They arrived back at headquarters to hear of more gunfire directed at her men.

"They was shooting at Hank and me out collecting," Mikey said. "I shot back and think I hit one of them."

"Who was it?" Helen asked.

"Some of the guys from the North Side."

"Shit. Why won't they leave us alone?" Helen asked.

"At least they didn't hit you," Kevin said.

"We ducked into a restaurant," Hank said. "But not before Mikey got some shots off."

"So it was a drive-by?" Helen asked.

"Yep."

"Shit," she repeated. Helen poured herself a drink and sat in a leather chair. She needed to formulate a plan. She knew her men depended on her to defend what was theirs.

"What are we gonna do?" Kevin asked.

"We're going to hurt them where it counts. In their pride. I want us to rob the Union Bank in the middle of their territory. Just to disrespect them."

"Who's gonna do it?"

"I want Hank and Mikey and Charlie and Floyd to take some men right now. Go."

The men left and the rest of them hung out and waited. Helen wished she could have gone with them, but knew it was too risky. She was playing her own game of cat and mouse with Moretti. She didn't need to have her face seen up north. Her men would represent her just fine.

Less than two hours later, the men were back and safe inside headquarters. Helen took their spoils and counted it.

"Good job, men. This was a good take." She entered the numbers in a ledger, then gave the men some cash to split with their crews.

Shots rang out from outside, and they heard screaming. Nothing hit their headquarters and Helen wondered what the point was.

Kevin grabbed Helen and took her to the farthest point from the door. Floyd opened the door and stood back, waiting to see if any more shots would come. When they heard silence, Floyd and Charlie walked outside. The neighborhood was deathly quiet. They grabbed Helen and walked around to see that the barbershop had been shot up.

"Was anyone hurt?" Floyd asked.

"No. No one was hit, but they shot this place up good," one of the older barbers said.

"Take some guys and board up the window," Helen said. "Make sure any supplies are replenished. I want them to be able to keep working."

"Did you see who did this?" Floyd asked.

"No idea."

"You absolutely sure? Think hard. You didn't see nobody?"

"Nope. We were just sitting here shooting the bull and suddenly the window was being shot to shit. We didn't notice the car or nothing."

"Damn. That doesn't make me happy," Helen said.

"Well we're not really happy, either. In case you wondered."

"I get that."

Helen assessed how bad the damage was. There were bullet holes in the walls, the mirrors were cracked, and comb cleaners were shattered.

"Can you work like this?" she asked.

"We can. We'd rather not."

"You boys go with Hank to get your supplies replenished. We'll get someone in to fix the mirrors. You'll be good to go in just a couple of hours."

She walked back around to headquarters.

"Charlie, you go over to Griswald's and get some mirrors. I want them installed this afternoon."

Charlie and several men left. Helen fumed. She felt helpless not knowing who'd attacked the sanctity of the barbershop. The message was clear, but it would be ignored. She wasn't about to back down on any front. She just wished she knew which gang she needed to go after next.

"It could have been the North Side retaliating for the robbery," Mikey said.

"It could also have been Capone's group. Moretti has a hard-on for you," Kevin said.

"So what do we do now?" Floyd rejoined the group.

"For now, we do nothing. I'll come up with a plan, but it will have to be later. How are the plans going for hitting Moretti's gambling tournament?"

"We're all set for that," Mikey said. "We're gonna kick their asses that night."

"Good. Now we need to come up with a big hit on Weiss's men."

"Or we can lay low for a while and wait for the heat to ease up," Kevin said.

"We're going to lay low for right now. But we'll get them. No one does this to us and gets away with it. I'm looking forward to a surprise attack."

"We're just lucky no one died today," Kevin said.

"And we had a successful bank hit. It's been a good day. Don't focus on the bad, Kevin."

"I suppose you're right," Kevin said.

"Keep that in mind. I'll be back," Helen said.

She drove to her apartment and called Maria.

"Hey, baby," Maria said.

"How you doin'?" Helen said.

"Good. How's your day going?"

"It's been another rough one. You want to get together for some dinner?"

"Sure. I'd like that. I have to be home by eight, though."

Helen was silent, fuming over the fact that Maria still belonged to Moretti and she had to be home to go out with him.

"Baby? You still there?" Maria asked.

"I'm here."

"I'm sorry."

"It's okay. It's the way it is right now."

"You just have to say the word and it will change," Maria said.

"I know."

"So what time shall we go to dinner?"

"Why don't I pick you up in thirty?"

"I'll be ready."

Helen arrived exactly thirty minutes later, and Maria came out of the house looking gorgeous in a black dress. Her outfit complemented Helen's black suit and tie. They drove to a steakhouse on the West Side. Helen opened Maria's car door for her and took her hand as they walked in.

She pulled her seat out for her and sat across from her, surveying the restaurant and seeing a good crowd. It was nice being in a safe, comfortable place with a beautiful date.

"You look amazing tonight," she said.

"Thanks, baby."

The waiter brought Helen's favorite red wine and poured some for her to taste. She nodded and he poured them each a glass. When he was out of sight, Helen raised her glass to Maria.

"To us," she said.

"To us," Maria said.

Helen looked into Maria's dark eyes and longed to be alone with her.

"What are you thinking, baby?" Maria asked.

"Just enjoying being with you."

"You're such a sweetheart."

Helen took a sip of wine just as the waiter came back for their orders. She ordered steaks for both of them and handed the waiter their menus. She tried to stay in the present, but couldn't help thinking that Maria would be out with Moretti later on.

"So what are you and Franco up to this evening?"

"I don't know. Probably Gattino's. Do you really care?"

"Call it morbid curiosity."

"I'd rather be with you."

"I'd rather you be with me, too," Helen said.

"Can we see each other tomorrow?"

"I'd like that."

Dinner arrived and they enjoyed it in quiet conversation. When they finished, Helen checked her pocket watch. It was seven o'clock.

"I'd better get you home."

She carefully looked around the neighborhood as they drove up. She saw no sign of trouble, so she parked and walked Maria to the door.

"Will you come in for a few minutes?" Maria asked.

"Sure. I'd like that."

She followed Maria down the hall to her room. Maria was quickly in her arms, her face turned up, looking at Helen. Helen bent and kissed her full lips. The kiss quickly intensified and Helen's head was soon light from passion. She ran her hands over the soft fabric of Maria's dress, itching to take it off and enjoy the body beneath.

She was aware of the time, though, and forced herself to pull away.

"I should let you get ready for your night."

"I wish you'd let me break it off with Franco."

"Soon, doll. We'll do that soon."

Chapter Thirteen

Lucky's was jumping the next time Kevin and Helen stopped by. The bullet holes were filled, and a whole new shipment of booze had arrived. Several of the couples in the speakeasy were smoking hashish and Helen just grinned, knowing how the sale of the weed lined her pockets.

One of the working girls came out to their table and tried her best to get Kevin to dance with her. Kevin had nothing to do with her, so Helen danced a few dances with her.

"Come on upstairs with me," the girl cooed in Helen's ear.

"No thanks, doll. You're here for the paying customers tonight."

"But I'd love a chance with you. I bet you know how to make a dame feel good."

"You're right about that." Helen laughed. "But you'll have to work up one of the men, if you want company tonight."

She sat back down and was surprised to see Mickey O'Leary walk in. He got a drink at the bar then joined them at the table.

"Mickey, it's good to see you," Helen said. "How's business?"

"It's great. I had to check this place out. I can't believe I've never been here."

She noticed Kevin was extremely quiet, looking downright uncomfortable. She excused herself, claiming she needed a new drink.

She watched the men from the bar and noted the tension between them. She wondered why Kevin had a problem with Mickey being there. Her thoughts were interrupted when Maria walked in.

Helen quickly crossed to her.

"What are you doing here?"

"Franco was being an ass, so I told him I wanted to go home. I took a cab to the Beaver, but you weren't there, so I took a chance and came here."

"Well, I'm glad you're here," Helen said. "Let me buy you a glass of wine."

They took their drinks back to their table, where Kevin and Mickey were finally having an easy conversation. Helen set their drinks on the table and led Maria to the dance floor. They moved to the music and Maria whispered in Helen's ear.

"Take me to your office, baby."

Helen led the way up the back stairs and to her office. Maria wrapped her arms around Helen's neck and pulled her close.

"I've missed you."

"I've missed you, too, doll." She slid her arms around Maria's waist before kissing her tenderly. "I've missed this a lot."

"I know you've been busy, but I still wish you'd call."

"It's only been a few days."

"It seems like so much longer." She kissed Helen again with all the passion that was pent up inside her.

Helen kissed her back, feverish in her need.

"We should get out of here," she said.

"Lead the way."

Helen took her hand and they left the bar, walking to Helen's apartment a few blocks away.

"I can't get over the view you have from here." Maria looked out over the cityscape.

Helen moved behind Maria and wrapped her arms around her. The view was stunning, but Helen had promised herself when she left the orphanage that she would only have the finest things in her life. The view and the woman in her arms were two of those.

She nuzzled the back of Maria's neck, then craned her neck to look down the top of her dress.

"I like this view, too."

"You cad." Maria playfully slapped at Helen's hand.

Helen laughed, then rested her head on Maria's shoulder.

"So what did Moretti do to get your goose tonight?"

Maria turned to face Helen. "Must we talk about him?"

"Not if you don't want to."

"I can think of things I'd rather do."

Helen kissed her slowly and deliberately. She slipped her tongue in Maria's mouth and explored at her leisure. When the kiss ended, Maria rested her head on Helen's chest and struggled to catch her breath.

Helen guided her to the couch and lay down. She pulled her on top of her and kissed her again, running her fingers through Maria's hair.

"You're so beautiful," she said.

"You make me feel beautiful."

"You always should."

Helen pulled Maria's mouth to hers. She moved her hands down her back to cup her ass.

"You've got the nicest body," Helen murmured against her lips.

"You say the sweetest things."

"I say the truth."

Helen kissed her again and ran her hands back up to cover Maria's breasts.

"I will say you're highly overdressed."

Maria stood and stripped off her clothes. Helen gazed at the naked beauty before her.

Helen joined her and held her briefly in her arms before she stepped out of her own clothes. When they were both undressed, Helen lay Maria on the couch and gently settled on top of her.

"Is there a reason we're not in the bedroom?" Maria asked.

"I thought you liked the view from here."

"I do." Maria ran her hands over Helen's body. "But wouldn't the bed be more comfortable?"

"You don't like this couch?"

"I don't like all this talk."

Helen kissed her as she dragged her hand along Maria's curves. She paused to knead a breast before squeezing her nipple. She moved her hand lower and slid her fingers inside.

"Oh yes," Maria cried.

Helen moved her fingers in and out as she watched the pleasure on Maria's face. She watched her face contort as she slipped her fingers out to caress her hard clit. Maria looked beautiful as she screamed Helen's name when the orgasms claimed her.

When Maria could breathe, she wiggled out from under Helen and stood.

"Now we go to the bedroom."

They lay together on the bed, with Maria curled against Helen. She was lazily running her fingers along Helen's body. Helen's nerves sang wherever she was touched. She opened her legs, willing Maria's fingers to work their magic there.

Maria rolled onto Helen and kissed her, her arm snaking between them so she could reach the heaven between Helen's legs.

Helen gasped at the sensation. She arched her back to press herself more fully into Maria, whose fingers were nimbly stroking her clit. Helen moved against her in time, and together, they brought her to a climax that made her head spin.

Helen lay gasping for breath for only a moment before she climbed between Maria's legs. She dipped to taste her, relishing again the flavor that was all her. She moved her tongue all over, devouring every inch, while Maria ground into her.

Helen focused her attention on Maria's clit, and in no time, Maria was reeling from more orgasms.

Maria pulled Helen up and snuggled into her arms. They lay there peacefully until the distinct sound of a tommy gun disturbed them.

"What was that?" Maria asked.

Helen was up and getting dressed.

"Shit! You stay here. I'm gonna head downstairs and see what's happening."

"Will that be safe? That sounded like gunfire."

"I'm sure it was. Let me go see what got hit."

"I'm going with you," Maria said.

"No, you're not. You're staying here where it's safe. I'll be right back."

She kissed Maria and took the elevator down to the ground floor. Gun pulled, she eased out the front door and down the street. There was a commotion closer to Lucky's.

"What happened?" Helen called to Kevin.

"Shots fired down the street."

"Not at us?"

"We haven't figured that out yet. I don't think so."

"Okay. Spread the men around and find out everything you can," Helen said. "I'll talk to you tomorrow."

She hurried back to her apartment and found Maria dressed and sitting on the couch, arms wrapped around herself.

"Hey, doll. You're okay."

"I'm scared. I was terrified and you left me."

"I had to go see what happened," Helen argued.

"Or you could have stayed with me."

"No, I couldn't have. I needed to make sure my men were fine. You're here. I could see you're alive. Scared, sure, but alive. I didn't know if my men were. I needed to go see."

"I'm sorry, baby. I don't want to fight."

"Well, you sure have a funny way of showing that."

"I was upset." She stood and moved into Helen's arms.

"You sure you're all right, then?"

"I am. I was just so scared, then you beat it out of here like a hero, and I didn't know if I'd ever see you again."

Helen brushed a tear off Maria's cheek.

"I'm always careful. You need to know that. You need to trust me."

"I do trust you. It's the other guys I worry about."

Helen laughed as she held Maria tight.

"Don't worry about them, either. I can hold my own."

"I hope so."

Helen held her for a few more minutes before realizing that she needed to get Maria home.

"Come on, doll. Let's call for a taxi and we'll get you home."

"Can't I stay with you here tonight?"

"I don't know how safe this neighborhood is tonight. We'll get you home where we won't have to worry about at least one gang. I'm sure you'll be fine at your boarding house."

They rode to the house, holding hands. When they arrived, Helen walked her to the door and hugged her tight.

"Make sure to lock the door behind you," Helen said. "I'll call you tomorrow."

"Be careful tonight. Take care of yourself."

Helen waited until she heard the door lock into place.

She turned and took the cab to her apartment closest to headquarters.

The next morning, Helen was already at headquarters when Kevin arrived.

"What did we learn last night?" she asked.

"They were shooting at Donovan's. That restaurant does some good business and is very generous with us, boss. They shot it up but good."

"Was anyone hurt?"

"No. The place was closed at that hour. But the message came through loud and clear."

"Yeah, they want us to back down. That ain't happening."

"What do you want from us, Helen?"

"What do you mean? I want us to go about our business, growing and making money. I don't see anyone complaining about that."

"I know you get tired of me harping on it, but people are dying here, boss."

"We don't know if it's Northsiders or the Outfit. We can't be sure these are Moretti's men. So back off Maria. She's not going anywhere."

"Fine. So who are we going to retaliate against?"

"I haven't decided. Both would be nice."

"I don't like being in a war with the North if there's no reason for it."

"And I don't see any reason to keep pissing off Capone if it's not them, but we can't sit idly by and let guys shoot up our territory and do nothing about it."

"So we go after them both?"

"Not yet. I need you to tap into your sources out there. I want you to get to the bottom of this. I want to know for sure who was behind it before we go running off half-cocked."

Kevin poured them each a cup of coffee. He sat across the table from Helen.

"What do you think we'll get out of all this?"

"That's a deep question, Kevin."

"Look, it's all fun and games when we're making a ton of money and guys aren't shooting at us twenty-four seven. But that ain't the way things are right now. What do we hope to gain from all this? We gonna expand? Take over some of their turf? What?"

"All I want is respect," Helen said. "All I want is to be able to go about my business and *not* get shot at all the time. I'm not thinking of taking over anyone's territory. But I also don't want them to see me as a sitting duck. Just sitting here waiting for them to pick me off. I don't like that, and I intend to show them we're not going to take this lying down."

"I guess I just feel like we're in a giant circle. We shoot back. They shoot again. So we shoot back and they shoot again. Where does it end?"

"It ends when they get more interested in each other and less interested in us again. That'll happen. Soon they'll realize we're small fish, and the real money lies with their worst enemies, each other."

"How do we get them to focus on each other again?" Kevin asked.

"We just have to be patient, my friend. It'll happen sooner than you think."

The morning passed quickly, and soon it was time for Kevin to go collect protection money from their businesses. Helen agreed to meet him at Mickey's for an early lunch.

She arrived at eleven thirty and found Kevin barely able to sit still.

"What's going on with you?" she asked.

"I can't believe you didn't hear what happened." He nearly bounced out of his chair.

"What did I miss?"

"Capone beat the shit out of Mayor Klenha."

"Cicero's mayor?"

"That's him. I guess he said something about running his office without the help of gangsters or some shit so Capone beat him unconscious."

"Damn. That man's got balls."

"Big ol' balls."

Mickey blushed as he approached with their food.

"I hope I'm not interrupting anything personal."

"Not at all," Helen said.

When Mickey was out of earshot, Helen asked, "So were the cops called?"

"Are you kidding me? They were there and didn't touch Capone."

"The man gets away with anything."

"Yeah, he does. You sure we want to go after him right now?"

"Maybe we'll lay low. But only for a while. Just to see how this plays out."

Chapter Fourteen

Helen sat in her headquarters, trying to focus on numbers, but her mind constantly drifted to Maria. She needed to see her. Work had kept her busy for a few days, and that was too long to be without the comforts she offered.

She was about to call her when Charlie burst through the door.

"What's going on?" Helen asked.

"They shot one of Capone's men point-blank," Charlie said.

"Who did?"

"Someone from the North Side. They walked up to Scarzoni on the street and pulled the trigger. He dropped right there. They killed the sucker from the North on the spot, but the guys from the South are pissed! Can you imagine the balls it took to do that in broad daylight?"

"When did it happen?"

"Just now. A couple of hours ago, maybe."

Helen smiled, thinking this just might be what she needed to take the heat off of her for a while.

"That's great news," she said. "Let's celebrate at Lucky's."

The place wasn't open when they got there, so she had Kevin bust out the booze and pour drinks for the ten or so men who were there. She then excused herself and went to her office, where she quickly called Maria.

"Hello?" came the soft voice on the other end.

"Hey, doll, how you doin'?" Helen asked.

"Good! I've missed you."

"I've missed you. Can I see you this afternoon?"

"Not this afternoon. How about tomorrow?"

Helen fought to keep the disappointment from her voice.

"Tomorrow would be great. I'll pick you up for lunch at noon."

"I'll be waiting."

"Sounds good, doll. I'll see you then."

"Good-bye, Helen."

Helen joined the men and reveled in the jubilant atmosphere. It was nice to be able to relax and enjoy themselves as opposed to being on alert all the time. With things heating up between the North and the South, they should be able to breathe a little easier, at least for a little while.

She relaxed with them, savoring her bourbon and pondering her next move. In less than a week, they'd hit Moretti's big gambling tournament. That would be enough retaliation for any of the hits the Outfit had been involved in lately. As far as the North went, Helen reasoned, they'd leave Helen and her crew alone as long as they stayed focused on Capone. Life was good for her.

❖

The next day at noon, Helen waited in front of the boarding house for Maria. Soon it was five after, then ten after. Helen was getting more and more nervous, sitting in the South's territory unprotected for that long.

Finally, Maria came down the front walk.

"Where have you been?" Helen demanded.

"Sorry, I was on the phone." Maria leaned in and kissed Helen's cheek.

"Who with?"

"Does it matter?"

"Maybe."

"Maybe it shouldn't," Maria said.

"Was it Moretti?" Helen asked.

"Yes, it was."

"I waited out here, a sitting duck for ten minutes, while you're on the phone with *Moretti*?"

"Baby, just say the word and I'll tell him where to go. If you insist on me pretending that I'm still his girl, I have to act the part."

"That's true. Sorry I got upset. You were doing what you had to do."

"Exactly."

"Let's get some food."

Helen took her to a seafood restaurant in her neighborhood. She ordered for both of them, including the white wine.

Maria smiled a lazy smile at Helen.

"What?" Helen asked.

"I kind of like it when you get jealous."

"When was I jealous?"

"When were you jealous?" Maria laughed. "When I was on the phone with Franco earlier."

"I wasn't jealous. I was boiling."

"I think you were jealous."

"I was sitting, unprotected, for ten minutes. That's not smart of me in that neighborhood. And to find out it was all because you were on the phone with Moretti set me off. I'm not jealous of that nobody."

"Says you."

Helen laughed. "Believe what you want, my dear, but can we change the subject?"

"Sure, baby. What do you want to talk about?"

"How about what I'm going to do to you after lunch?"

Maria blushed.

"You're too easy," Helen teased her.

"We'll see how easy I am," Maria said.

Helen laughed. "You gonna play hard to get?"

"Maybe I am."

"Too late, doll."

"Hey, that's not nice."

"I'm gonna make you scream my name before you even get comfortable," Helen whispered. "I'm going to peel your clothes off with my teeth and lick you from head to toe."

Maria was a deep burgundy and squirmed in her seat.

"Helen!" she said. "People can hear."

"I'm being quiet. Only you and I know what I'm saying. You need to relax."

Maria looked around while Helen softly chuckled. No one seemed to be paying them any attention, and she fumed a little that Helen was right.

"Are you ever wrong about anything?" she asked.

"I try not to be."

"You're so smug," Maria said.

"No, just right."

Lunch was served and Helen quit teasing Maria so she could enjoy her food. After they ate, Helen drove them to her apartment and quickly took Maria in her arms.

She kissed her with all the passion she'd been saving for days. She kissed her hard, plunging her tongue inside her mouth and tasting the warm moistness she found. She pulled Maria against her, running her hands up and down her sides, finally bringing her hands to stop on her breasts. She slid one hand under her dress to cup a breast through her bra. Her breath caught as she felt the nipple harden at her touch.

"Help me out of this," Maria begged her.

Helen was more than happy to unzip the dress and let it fall to the floor. Maria unhooked her bra and tossed it on her dress.

Helen moved her hand between Maria's legs, but Maria grabbed her hand. "I believe you said something about kissing every inch of me."

"That I did." Helen deftly removed Maria's panties and threw them on the pile of discarded clothes. She then peeled her stockings off with her teeth.

"Is that what you were thinking?"

"That's a good start," Maria said.

Helen eased Maria onto the bed and moved to her feet. She took one and slowly, deliberately sucked her big toe into her mouth, running her tongue all over it.

"Oh, my God," Maria gasped.

Helen repeated her actions with every toe on that foot before moving to the next one. She sucked and licked those toes before kissing up to her ankle. She lazily dragged her tongue over the ankle and kissed and nibbled her way up the calf.

Maria was squirming on the bed. Helen was beyond aroused herself, but cautioned herself to stay focused and fulfill her promise to Maria. She finally reached the back of Maria's knee, which she sucked and nipped at. She licked the soft skin before continuing her oral assault up the tender skin of her inner thigh.

Maria pressed her hand into the back of Helen's head as Helen kissed closer and closer to her center. She arched her back and tried to guide Helen to where she needed her most. Helen lightly kissed her clit before kissing down her other thigh. She could feel the heat radiating from Maria and wanted nothing more than to bury her tongue deep inside. She was dizzy with need as she kissed to the back of Maria's other knee and dragged her tongue over the sensitive skin she found there.

As she kissed down her shapely calf, she asked herself if she'd be able to continue this. Would she have the fortitude to kiss everywhere but where she knew Maria wanted her? She kissed back up her leg and this time briefly dipped her tongue inside. She forced herself away and nibbled her way up Maria's soft belly to her breasts. Her nipples were so hard, they looked painful.

She closed her mouth around one, pulling it deep into her mouth, feeling the nipple press into the roof of her mouth. She straddled Maria's leg and ground into her. She sucked on the other nipple, lost in her desire to please Maria.

When she could barely take any more torture, she kissed Maria's mouth. She moved her tongue all around, frantically mimicking the action she longed to do between her legs.

Maria took her hand and placed it on her center.

"Please, baby."

Helen was happy to oblige. She slid her fingers easily inside Maria. She coated them with her cream then rubbed her swollen clit. Maria moved against her hand, obviously close to her climax. Helen smiled as she sucked on her nipple, pleased with herself for getting Maria so worked up.

Maria put her own hand over Helen's and helped her rub until her breath caught and her body froze, the climax crashing through her.

Helen stood and quickly stripped out of her clothes, anxious to feel the relief that Maria would give her. She lowered herself over Maria's face and fought to maintain control as Maria's tongue worked its magic. Helen felt the ball of heat forming at her center. She felt it explode, sending waves of heat over every inch of her body.

She climbed off Maria and pulled her close.

"So when can I tell Franco to get lost?" Maria asked.

"Soon, doll. In another week or so, you'll leave him for good. I promise." Helen thought of the hit they were planning on the gambling tournament. She hoped they'd take Moretti out then and Maria would be free of him for good.

"I hope so," Maria said. "I hate being around him when I'd much rather be with you."

"I know. Don't worry. It'll be just us soon."

Chapter Fifteen

A few days passed before Helen was able to call Maria. "Hey, doll, can I come over and see you?"

"Sure. Come on by."

Helen arrived and pulled Maria into her arms.

"I've missed you."

"I've missed you, too. I want to see you more often. This every few days isn't working for me."

Helen was about to respond when the sound of gunfire erupted. Helen pulled Maria to the floor and lay on top of her until it quieted. They heard a car take off.

"What was that about?" Maria said.

"I don't know. They didn't hit anything in here. You stay here I'll go outside and look around."

Helen cautiously opened the door and backed away, fearing more gunshots. Hearing none, she ventured outside. The building looked fine. She closed the door and went back to Maria.

"I don't see anything. I don't know what they were shooting at, but they didn't seem to hit anything. Maybe they were just warning shots."

"I'm sorry, baby. We knew this wouldn't be easy."

"True. But I'm not backing down."

Maria closed the distance between them and wrapped her arms around Helen, who held her tight.

"You're something special, Helen."

"So are you, Maria."

Helen broke the embrace. "I need to get to work. I'll be back later. We'll have dinner."

"That would be swell."

Helen kissed her and left. She reached her car and stopped in her tracks. It listed horribly to the right. She walked around it and found it was riddled with bullet holes.

"Shit!" She looked around the empty street. She was safe, but her car was ruined. She walked back up to the house. Maria opened the door.

"I was watching you. What's wrong?"

"They shot up my car. I need to use your phone."

"It's in the hall."

Helen called headquarters and was relieved when Kevin answered.

"They got my car," she said. "I need you to come get me."

"Where are you?" he asked.

"Shit. I'm at a boarding house on the South Side." She gave him the address.

"And just what are you doing there?"

"What the fuck do you think? Just get here." She slammed down the phone.

Kevin arrived and Helen got in the car. They rode in silence for a few minutes.

"Boss, are you sure you know what you're doing?"

"It's none of your business, Kevin."

"They're not going to stop 'til you're dead."

"They don't want me dead. They just want me to back off."

"You don't know that."

"They're not going to kill me over a girl."

"Look, boss, you don't know how Moretti feels about this gal. He might really love her."

"He doesn't deserve her."

"That's not for you to decide."

They returned to headquarters and Kevin got on the phone to call a truck to tow Helen's car. Helen was in a foul mood. She couldn't get over the nerve of Moretti's people shooting her car in broad daylight.

"What time are the boys hitting the gambling hall tonight?" she asked Kevin.

"They're gunning for midnight."

"Good. I hope they draw blood."

"You know this could turn into a war because you're hot for some hussy."

"She's not a hussy, and don't you ever call her that again."

"God, boss. Listen to yourself. Men could die over this."

"As long as they're Moretti's men, I don't care. Now take me to Hank's. I need a new car."

❖

Helen picked Maria up at six o'clock. She was on alert for anything out of the ordinary, anyone who looked suspicious. She saw nothing, but drove away with a heavy sigh of relief.

"Franco's going to wonder where I am," Maria said as Helen steered them to a safer part of town.

"I'm sure he knows," Helen said.

"Are you scared?"

"No. I'm steamed."

"But what if you'd been in your car this afternoon?"

"I wasn't. And they knew that."

They arrived at a steakhouse Helen owned on the West Side. They dined in peace, knowing they were safe. For the moment.

"Maybe we should get out of town for a while," Helen said.

"Where would we go?"

"I've got a place up in Wisconsin. It's on the lake. We could lay low for a few days."

"Are you serious?"

Helen sighed. "I don't think I am. As nice as it sounds, I really need to be here for the guys right now."

"You're not taking Franco's crap lying down are you?"

"That's not something for you to worry about, doll."

"What? I'm not good enough to discuss business with?"

"That's not it. I just don't like to talk about business when I'm with you. Especially this mess with Moretti."

Maria pouted. Helen ran her thumb over her extended bottom lip.

"It drives me crazy when you do that. It makes me want to suck on that lip."

"Why don't you?"

"Let's get out of here."

Helen drove to her apartment and once inside, she quickly took Maria in her arms. She kissed her hard, stripping her dress off her. Her breath caught at the sight of Maria standing in her lingerie. She closed her hand around a pert breast and rubbed the nipple through the flimsy material as she kissed her more passionately.

Maria fumbled with the buttons on Helen's shirt, finally sliding it off and letting it fall to the floor. She moved her hands to Helen's chest. Helen took her hands and led her to the bedroom, where she eased her onto the bed.

"You're so beautiful," she whispered. She helped her out of her bra and panties and quickly stripped off the rest of her own clothes. When they met skin to skin, the electricity between them was palpable.

Helen moved her knee between Maria's legs as she nibbled her neck. She kissed down her neck, stopping to taste every inch, until she reached a taut nipple. She closed her mouth on it, drawing it in deep.

Maria arched against her, moving against her knee. Helen slid her hand between them and found Maria's clit slick and swollen. She teased it, rubbing circles around it until Maria begged for more.

"Please. Please, Helen."

Helen ran her fingers over Maria and was greeted with a shudder as Maria came on her hand. She waited until Maria's breathing steadied then started over again. It took little time before Maria cried out as another orgasm racked her body.

They made love for hours, with Helen taking Maria to one climax after another. Maria finally protested that she'd had enough and Helen lay back, pulling Maria close.

"I don't know how you do that," Maria said. "You make me feel so many different things."

"Good, doll. You should feel all those things. All the time. Now just relax."

"How could I do anything else?"

Helen lay awake as Maria slept in her arms. She knew she had to wake her up soon so she could get to headquarters. The hit would be happening any minute, and she wanted to be sure she was at the office when the men showed up.

"Hey, doll? Maria?" She kissed Maria's ear. "Time to wake up. I need to get you home."

"Hmm? Why? Can't we just stay here?"

"Not tonight. I've got some stuff to take care of. Come on. Get up and dressed so I can drive you home."

A groggy Maria rose and pulled herself together as Helen watched. She quickly dressed herself and they took the elevator to the main floor. Helen was vigilant as they left, once again. She needed to be sure no one was waiting to do either of them harm. Satisfied the coast was clear, she drove Maria home and dropped her off.

"I'll call you," she said.

"You promise?"

"I promise." She kissed Maria and watched her let herself into the boarding house. Knowing she was safe, Helen sped out of the neighborhood and back to the safety of her office.

❖

Helen arrived at the room behind the barbershop at just past midnight. She let herself in and poured herself a bourbon while she waited. Less than a half hour later, Kevin walked in, followed by the gang of men who'd hit Moretti's place. Helen jumped to her feet.

"How'd it go? Tell me what happened."

"That place is in shreds," one of her lieutenants said. "We shot it up but good."

"How many people were hit?" Helen asked.

"A lot," Kevin said. "But we shot fast and got the hell out of there so we didn't stick around to get a count."

"Any of ours get hit?"

"Not a one."

"Good job, men," Helen said.

"We shot the shit out of their booze, too," another commented.

"Sounds like a successful mission. Let's drink."

Drinks were poured all around. The atmosphere was euphoric. Kevin pulled Helen aside.

"Moretti was there, but not his girl. You know anything about that?"

"Maybe I made sure she was safe."

"You didn't tell her about the hit, did you?"

"What do you take me for?"

"I'm just checking, boss. You don't think right when it comes to that dame."

"What about you? You shouldn't have had time to notice she wasn't there. Where's your head?"

Kevin hung his head.

"I just don't want you compromising your safety or the safety of the men because you're worried about my relationship with Maria," Helen said. "Now let's get back to the party."

The celebration lasted into the wee hours of the morning. Helen congratulated herself on a great day as she drove home.

When she finally awoke the next morning, she was still in fine spirits and immediately called Maria.

"Hi, doll."

"Hi yourself. I heard what happened last night. I could have been killed."

Helen sat up in bed. "You think I would let that happen to you?"

"So that's all last night was? A way to keep me from being shot?"

"Maria, calm down. Last night was much more than that."

"I appreciate you keeping me safe, but I don't like that you used me like that. Was I your alibi?"

"I didn't use you. Last night was wonderful."

"Were you staring at the clock the whole time?" Maria said. "Waiting until it was safe to take me home?"

"That's not how it was at all."

"Bullshit!"

"What can I say to convince you?"

"I need some time. I don't know if this is worth it."

"What? You can't be serious."

"I am. Good-bye, Helen."

The line went dead.

"Dames!" Helen spat as she slammed down the receiver. She climbed out of bed and took a long shower, playing over every moment she'd spent with Maria. Frustrated and more annoyed than before, she got out and dressed quickly.

She arrived at headquarters to find several hungover men already there.

"What's going on?" She poured herself a bourbon.

"Capone got a shipment last night." The young man's voice quaked as he said it.

"So?"

"So you told us to hit it," another said.

"Oh, yeah," Helen shook herself out of her misery and focused on current matters. "We hit the gambling hall last night. We'll hit the shipment another time."

The men looked at each other, then back to Helen.

"So the next shipment will be okay with you?"

"Sure."

"You okay?" one of them asked.

"Of course," she snapped.

"We thought you'd be mad as hell."

"Last night was a job well done. No need to get upset over the missed shipment. We weren't anywhere near ready to hit it anyway. How many guns does he have riding with it? What's their route?"

"We don't know all that yet."

"Then it would have been like lambs being led to slaughter. I want you guys to do your research and get back to me when we know what it's going to take. I don't want to lose any men when it happens."

Kevin walked in and took one look at Helen.

"You're at it early."

"Don't judge."

"I was just commenting."

"Well, don't." To the rest of the men, she said, "Go make some collections and meet us at Mickey's in two hours."

They dispersed, leaving Kevin and Helen alone.

"You want to talk about it?" Kevin poured himself a drink.

"No."

"Fine. But you should know you look like shit."

"Nothing that work won't help."

"You want to make the rounds with me today?" he asked.

"Sure."

Helen's mood improved only slightly as their takes weren't as lucrative as she would have liked. By the time they got to

Mickey's, they'd hit ten establishments and their envelopes weren't as thick as usual.

"That's what happens when you're the ones involved in the war. No one wants to get shot up, so they avoid our businesses." Kevin glared at Helen.

"You know, Kevin, you're getting awfully big for your britches lately."

"I'm just worried, is all."

"Well, don't."

Mickey arrived with their lunches and Helen felt resentment toward the obvious feelings between Mickey and Kevin. When Mickey was out of earshot, Kevin got back to business.

"So what's our next move? We let Moretti have at us, or do we hit him again?"

"You don't need to worry about Moretti anymore. I'm sure he'll leave us be."

They heard squealing tires and the sounds of car doors slamming. They reached for their guns before three of their men ran in.

"Leo and Donnie got hit," one said.

"What? Where? Who?" Helen said.

"Over by Marigold's bakery. They had just picked up from them when some of Weiss's men shot 'em."

"How do you know?"

"We were meeting them. We were all going to drive over together."

"Where are they now?"

"On their way to General."

"Let's go." Helen lead the way to the front door. "How do you know it was guys from the North."

"I recognized DeSoto."

"Shit."

"We're taking heat from all sides. Real nice," Kevin said.

They found Leo in stable condition at the hospital, but were saddened to learn that Donnie hadn't made it.

"Shit," Helen repeated.

Chapter Sixteen

Ten men stood guard as Helen watched Donnie be lowered into the ground. It was a somber day and a reminder to them all how dangerous a business they were in. The funeral had been nice, and the whole gang had followed the hearse to the cemetery. As Helen turned away from the grave, her thoughts turned to Maria. Maybe she had been right. The price wasn't worth it. Although, she knew she didn't believe it. She wanted Maria. And she wasn't ready to give up just yet.

The gang agreed to meet at the Golden Beaver, opting to celebrate Donnie's life. It was their way of mourning. Helen rode with Kevin.

"You doin' okay, boss?"

"As well as I can be."

"It's part of life, you know. Death, I mean."

"That's very profound," Helen said.

"You don't have to be such a bitch."

"I'm sorry. That came out harsher than I meant it. I know it's part of life. But he was so young. Twenty-two is too young to die."

They rode in silence for a bit, then Helen said, "And why us? What the fuck did we do to draw Weiss's ire?"

"I don't know, boss. You're not sleeping with his girl, too, are you?"

"Fuck you."

They arrived at the speakeasy. Helen slammed her door as she got out. Kevin was quickly beside her.

"I'm sorry. That wasn't nice."

"Not nice? It was a shitty thing to say."

"I'm worried about you, Helen."

"Don't be. Maria and I are off. And I'm not sleeping with anyone from Hymie's group, either. Okay? Now forget about me and let's go think of Donnie."

The party got raucous and was going strong late into the night when Moretti walked in with Maria on his arm. Her men immediately grabbed their guns, but Moretti and Maria were followed by only a few men. They strolled back to Helen's table. She bit her tongue to keep from asking how he liked sloppy seconds.

"What are you doing here?" she said instead.

"I've come to offer my condolences. I heard what happened."

Helen motioned to an empty chair, noting that Maria was looking everywhere but at her.

"Do you know why the guys from the North wanted to get us?" she asked.

"No idea. You?"

"None."

"Maybe they just got tired of shooting at us," Moretti said.

"Who'd get tired of that?" Helen asked.

"Funny. That's another reason I'm here. What do you say we call a truce to our little feud? I'd say there's no reason for us to shoot each other up any more."

Helen seethed inside. So he had his girl back and didn't want Helen to fight for her. She'd be damned if she'd sit back and let him win. She wasn't about to admit that to him, though.

"Sounds fair," Helen said.

They shook hands and Helen saw Kevin breathe a sigh of relief. Damn him. Damn them all. She looked like a loser and she didn't like that. She would be the victor in the end. She knew that. It was just a matter of time. Let them all be smug for now.

One of the working girls managed to squeeze behind Helen's chair. She ran her hands over Helen's shoulders and down across her chest.

"What's a girl gotta do to get a dance with a handsome woman like you?"

Helen cringed inwardly. She wanted to hold Maria, to dance with that lithe, limber body. Still, she didn't want to be a sad sack.

"Just ask, doll." She stood. "Excuse us."

They danced several dances together. It felt good to Helen to move to the music.

"Why don't you come up and see me tonight?" the girl asked.

Tempting though it was, it wouldn't be Maria. Helen wasn't ready for that.

"Tonight's about a good man," Helen said. "Maybe some other time."

❖

The group at headquarters was somber, still reeling from Donnie's death. Helen worked quietly entering numbers into the ledger while her men sat around, some talking, some just staring into space.

"What now?" Charlie asked.

"Yeah. What next, boss?" Kevin said.

Helen was drained. She didn't want to fight any more. She just wanted to be left alone to do her business. She knew this was a price she was paying for firing back at both gangs when she didn't know who was behind the hits earlier. But she was tired of it. She wanted to kill Moretti and take Maria back, but she didn't want to mess with Hymie's gang in the North any longer.

Still, she knew she'd have to. Her men wouldn't respect her if she let Donnie's death go unanswered.

"We need to hit them back, obviously," Helen said. "Just give me some time to think. We'll come up with a solid hit. I don't want to lose any more men."

Mikey walked in and added more dismal news to their day.

"The Prohis are in town," he said, referring to agents from the Bureau of Prohibition.

"Where'd you hear that?" Helen asked.

"I heard they hit the Green Mill and Halligan's last night."

"No shit? Capone and Weiss must be fuming."

"I heard they're blaming each other for ratting the other one out. I don't know who squealed, but I'm sure there's going to be hell to pay."

"I wonder who told them about those places," Helen mused. "I'm just glad we weren't mentioned."

"Nope. No one suspicious was at the Beaver or Lucky's last night."

"Good. Let's hope that continues."

"Should we close them down for a few days, until the heat's gone?" Kevin asked.

"No. I think we're safe. We're small-time. No one's going to come after us."

The phone rang and Kevin answered it.

"Sure thing. Hold on a sec." He handed the phone to Helen.

"This is Helen."

"Hey, Helen," Mario the barber said. "There's some guy here asking to talk to you."

"Who is it?"

"He says he's with the Bureau, ma'am."

"Shit."

"What shall I tell him?"

"Tell him I'll be right there."

She hung up the phone.

"What's up, boss? You look like you've seen a ghost."

"The Prohis are here. I need to go meet with him. You guys lay low for a while, okay?"

She walked around to the barbershop. A man in a suit walked up.

"You must be Helen Byrne. I'm Agent Harold Waverly." He extended his hand, which Helen refused to take.

"What do you want with me, Agent Waverly?"

"Please call me Harold. Is there somewhere we can talk?"

"Anything you want to say to me, you can say right here."

"I think you'll regret that, Ms. Byrne. I'd rather talk to you privately."

"I've got nothing to say to you," Helen said. "If you've got something to say, say it now."

"I think you know that if we wanted to, we could shut you down and put you away for a long time."

"Says you."

"Says me. But we're after bigger fish. No offense."

"None taken."

"In order to catch those fish, we could use your help. In return, we'll look away from you."

"I'm not a rat."

"But are you a martyr? Are you willing to go to jail while they stay free?"

"I don't know anything about anyone, Agent. I couldn't help you even if I wanted to."

"I don't believe you."

"Believe me or don't believe me." Helen shrugged. "It doesn't change the fact that I know nothing."

"Maybe you want to make something up then? Anything to keep the heat off you? You know they wouldn't hesitate to sell you out."

"I'm sorry, Agent Waverly. I really am. But I don't have any information you might need. So if you'll excuse me."

She turned to leave, but froze when the agent spoke again.

"You sure about that? You don't know a woman named Maria Falco?"

"Nope. I don't know that name." She walked out, a cold pit of fear in her stomach.

"How did it go?" Kevin asked when she got back to headquarters,

"They wanted me to spill on one of the other gangs."

"And you didn't?"

"I'm not a rat," Helen said.

"So what does that mean for us?" Charlie asked.

"It means they say they're looking at us."

"That ain't good," Kevin said.

"They're after the big guys. They're not going to waste their time with us."

"I hope you're right. We don't need no trouble."

"They'll leave us alone. Trust me. But just to be sure, make some phone calls. I want Lucky's and the Beaver closed for the next few days. Until the heat's gone."

"Where will we hang out?"

"We'll lay low, too. I don't want any trouble from these guys."

"You said they'd leave us alone."

"And I think they will. But there's no reason to invite them to come sniffin' around us."

"They already are."

"Not really. I don't believe they want to bother us. They want information from us. That's all. And I don't want anyone squealing on anyone else. Do you understand me?"

They all nodded.

"Good. I don't expect these guys to be around long. They won't get anything and will be on their way soon."

Chapter Seventeen

Helen was restless. She didn't like laying low and knew her men were getting antsy, too. Kevin was particularly on edge.

"Hey, Kevin, why don't we head over to Gattino's?"

"Why?"

"Because I feel like blowing off some steam."

"Why support them? Why not just open Lucky's or the Beaver?"

"It's only been a few days. Give it a few more. As long as the Prohis are in town, we've got to lay low."

"So how do we know Gattino's will even be open?"

"We don't. But let's go try."

They hadn't been driving long when Helen spotted their tail.

"Shit," she said.

"What's up?"

"We're being followed."

"So what do I do?"

"Just drive me to my apartment over by Lucky's. No reason to lead them to Gattino's."

"Okay, boss, but wouldn't it be nice to turn Moretti over to them?"

"No. That would be suicide. I wouldn't cry if they caught him, but it's not going to be with my help."

She checked the mirror and saw the car still following.

"You want me to lose them?" Kevin asked.

"No. It's not worth it. Just drop me off and head home."

"You got it."

Helen paced back and forth in her apartment. It was too early for her to be home. She was tired of being good and laying low. She needed something to do but could think of nothing. What she really wanted to do was call Maria, but that wasn't going to happen. She'd called her a couple of times, but Maria hadn't taken her calls.

She wondered how Maria was doing and how Moretti was faring with the government in town. How she wished they'd arrest Moretti and throw away the key. Then she'd be free to have Maria to herself. But that hadn't happened.

She sat down and tried to plot a comeback against Hymie Weiss's men for killing Donnie. She needed to hit them hard. Her men expected it. She finally decided on a repeat of their previous drive-by.

❖

The next day, the men were lounging around headquarters, wishing they had something to do. They looked up expectantly when Helen finally arrived.

"I've got an idea," she said.

"What kind of idea?" Kevin asked.

"I want to hit some of Hymie's men. They killed Donnie. I want them to know we're not going to take it lying down."

"But with everyone lying low, how are we supposed to hit anyone?"

"Charlie, I want you to take some men and cruise the neighborhood by Schofield's again. Keep your eyes peeled for anyone who looks like they work for Weiss. Then shoot 'em. No questions asked. I want at least one dead. For Donnie. More would be better. Got it?"

"Got it, Helen. When do you want us to do this?"

"Now. Get out of here."

Charlie wrestled up a few men off couches and out of poker games and headed to the North Side of town.

Helen sat and played poker as she waited. She was so distracted that she lost the first few hands. Forcing herself to focus, she finally became a contender, winning most of the hands from then on.

It wasn't long before Charlie and his men returned.

"We shot five men," he announced.

"Yeah? Did you kill them?"

"I'm pretty sure. We couldn't really hang out since there were cops crawling all over. They chased us for a while, but we lost 'em."

"Good job. Do you think the people who saw you knew you were from our gang?"

"I'm pretty sure. Weiss's men were everywhere. They sure ain't lying low."

"Good. I want them to know we hit them back."

The men were drinking and everyone was relaxed when the phone rang.

"Yeah. Just a second." Kevin handed the phone to Helen.

"That agent guy is back," Mario said. "He wants to talk to you."

"Shit. I'll be right up."

She walked around to the barbershop.

"Agent Waverly. What a pleasant surprise."

"Spare me the sarcasm, Byrne. What happened today?"

"What are you talking about?"

"You've got balls for a woman. I've gotta give you that. There's federal agents everywhere in this town and you still execute a hit. I'm impressed."

"I'm afraid I don't know what you're talking about."

"Everyone knows it was your men who took out some of Weiss's men an hour or so ago."

"My men? I'm a bookkeeper for a barber. I'm afraid you give me too much credit, Agent Waverly."

"Bullshit. We've been watching you, and we're going to keep watching you. One false move and you're in the slammer."

"I'll mind my p's and q's." She turned to leave.

"I don't think I dismissed you."

"I told you the other day, I've got nothing to say to you."

"Watch yourself, Byrne. No one likes a wise guy."

Helen threw her head back and laughed. She was a wise guy and everyone loved her. He was so full of shit.

"I'll consider myself warned."

She walked back to headquarters and poured herself a drink.

"I'll be so fucking happy when the Prohis are out of here. I don't like them hanging around. They're cramping my style."

"What do they want from you now, boss?" Kevin asked.

"I'm not even sure. I mean, I know they want me to rat out the big boys, but today it was almost like he thought I'd admit to hitting Weiss's men. I don't know what he's thinking, but he's crazy if he thinks I'm saying one incriminating word to him, about myself or Weiss or Capone."

Helen left the men and drove to her apartment. She dialed Maria's number. The woman who answered said Maria didn't want to talk to her.

"Shit!"

Helen really missed Maria and wanted the opportunity to prove herself. But she had no way of doing that. She decided she had to take a chance. She drove back and picked up Kevin.

"We're going to Gattino's," she said.

"Why?"

"I want to know how hot the heat is right now. Waverly can't be the only game in town."

"You sure that's what you want?"

"I'm sure."

They walked in to the quiet speakeasy, noting that the Prohis' presence wasn't just hurting her and her men.

"Slow night?" she said to Moretti.

"The slowest."

"Hey, doll," she said to Maria. "How you doin'?"

Maria looked at her fingernails, apparently lost in admiring them.

"So, what? You're not talking to me?"

Maria leveled a glare at her, but said nothing.

Moretti laughed.

"You girls have a falling out or something?"

"Or something, I guess," Helen said before changing the subject. "So how hot's it gonna get, Moretti? Have you heard how long the Prohis are gonna be here?"

"I haven't heard. Have they been talkin' to you?"

"They're tryin' to. I'm not giving them anything."

"Smart woman."

"Are they leaning on you guys pretty hard?"
"They're sniffin' around. They're not getting anything."
"Shit. I wish they'd fuckin' leave already."
"You still operating your places?" Moretti asked.
"Nah. We're closed for a few days."
"Smart." Moretti nodded.

Helen felt how small she really was at that moment. If the Prohis closed down Gattino's, Capone and his men still had dozens of speakeasies. If they closed one of hers, she'd take a hard hit financially.

She made her mind up then to reopen Lucky's. At least she'd have some income. She'd have the guys watching the door be hyper vigilant. That decision was followed by the decision that she needed to get out of there. She needed to get as far away from Maria as possible. She obviously didn't want to have anything to do with Helen, and that hurt.

"Thanks for the information." She stood.
"Wish I had better news for you."
"Me, too. Good luck."
"Yeah, Helen. You, too."
"Well? That was a waste of time, huh?" Kevin said when they were in the car again.
"Not completely."
"No?"
"No. I've decided to reopen Lucky's. If they can keep their places open, we can do the same. At least with one. I have to believe the Prohis aren't really interested in me."
"That's a gutsy call, Helen."
"Tomorrow, I want you to get the word out that it's gonna reopen. I don't care if there's not a huge crowd, but I want people to know we're alive and kickin' right now."
"You got it, boss."

❖

The next night, Helen and Kevin and a few of the guys were at Lucky's. They weren't alone, but it was a subdued crowd. Helen wanted to see people let loose and party.

"Kevin, give a little hashish away. Not a lot, but a little. Get people happy."

He left to circulate. Helen and her men continued to people watch as they drank. One of the working girls walked up behind Helen and tossed her leg around her, her foot landing on her chair between her legs. She leaned forward and whispered in Helen's ear.

"Hey good lookin'."

"Hey yourself." She leaned back and rested her head on the woman's ample bosom.

The woman ran her hands up and down Helen's chest.

"We've missed you upstairs," she said.

"I like to think you've been busy enough without me up there," Helen said.

"Yeah, but no one treats us as well as you do."

Helen laughed. She enjoyed the women who enjoyed women. She felt sorry for them, having to sleep with men all the time, but that was their job.

"It's a slow night, boss lady," the woman said. "Why don't you come upstairs and have some fun?"

Helen thought long and hard about the offer. The comfort the woman could provide would be sorely welcomed. She could get her mind off the Prohis, the gang wars, and Maria. Maria. She wouldn't be able to get her off her mind, no matter how talented this woman was. Maria would be the one she was thinking of, and that wouldn't be fair to anyone. Damn, she hated that woman.

"Thanks anyway, and maybe next time, but you need to work the crowd. See if you can drum up some business."

"All right, gorgeous, but don't say I didn't offer."

They were watching her walk off when there was a commotion at the door. In walked Waverly and his men, showing their badges and telling everyone to put their hands on their heads.

They rounded everyone up, including Helen, and locked them in a paddy wagon. When they arrived at the station, Helen was placed in an interrogation room.

"You want out of here?" Waverly walked in the room.

"Sure."

"Tell me about Big Al. Give me something to go on and you're free."

"I've got nothing. I don't know anything that can help you."

"Try me."

"No."

"Then you'll stay here." He called a guard to escort her to the holding cell.

She waited with her girls and several of the patrons. The same woman who hit on her earlier came over and sat next to her.

"Hey, sunshine. This is exciting, huh?"

Helen had to laugh.

"That's one way of looking at it."

"How long until they spring us?" the woman asked.

"It shouldn't be long. I'm sure Kevin's got people on their way now."

"For you. What about the rest of us?"

"If you work for me, I'll spring you. Don't worry."

"Thanks, boss lady."

Less than an hour later, Helen's men had posted bail for her and her employees.

"Can I ride with you?" The working woman was at Helen's elbow.

"Sure. We'll drop you off at your place."

They climbed in the backseat of Charlie's car while Kevin joined Charlie in the front.

The woman sidled close to Helen and placed her hand on her knee. Helen enjoyed the contact and placed her hand over the woman's.

"So, do you have a name?"

"Carol."

"Hi, Carol. It's nice to meet you."

"You're a very handsome woman, you know, Helen Byrne." She pressed her breasts against Helen.

"And you're quite a charmer, Carol."

"Sorry if I forget my manners around you. I get distracted."

"It's quite all right. You're very refreshing."

"Yeah? I'd like to show you how refreshing I can be." She kissed Helen's neck and sucked on her earlobe.

Helen drew her breath at the sensation. Her crotch clenched in response.

"We're here," Charlie said. "At Carol's place."

"Please come up with me," Carol whispered.

Temptation roared through Helen. Carol was a voluptuous, sensual woman who clearly wanted nothing more than a good time. Helen deserved a good time. It had been a rough week. But logic won out.

"I'm sorry, doll. I'd love to, but I need to keep a clear head right now with everything going on. I need to think things through. Thank you, though. And maybe next time."

She pulled Carol to her and kissed her. It was a soft kiss, yet passionate. Helen's frustration apparent in it.

"Good night, Helen."

"Good night, Carol."

Charlie drove Helen around to her apartment. She said her good nights and entered her place alone. Lonely and exhausted, she stripped down and climbed into bed. Her mind replayed the events of the past few days. She needed to come up with a way to deal with Waverly. She needed to figure out how to make more money now that Lucky's was shut down.

She closed her eyes and her last thoughts were of Maria before she fell into a tormented sleep.

Chapter Eighteen

"They're saying you fingered them," Kevin said to Helen over coffee.

"I would never give them up," Helen said, referring to one of Moretti's clubs having been busted by the Prohis.

"That's not what they think. They say you saved your own ass by pointing to them."

"Shit. They'll be all over us again now."

"Yeah, they will."

"We'll need to have everyone be extra careful now. No telling when they'll hit."

The hit never came, and three weeks later, the agents were gone, with no further casualties. Helen was pissed that her speakeasy was one of the four that was busted, and she was still paranoid about the South retaliating against her.

"Be careful out there," she told her men. "We're sitting ducks right now. The agents are gone, so it's back to work, but with no agents watching them, the South should be gunning for us. Please watch your backs and have someone with you all the time while you're working. No goin' solo right now."

Following her own orders, Helen joined Kevin and two other men as they collected that day. They picked up hefty envelopes as people had started frequenting the businesses since the shootings had settled down while the agents were in town.

Helen was in good spirits as they drove back to headquarters. They were almost there when the shots rang out. The sound of the tommy guns roared even over the sound of the car. Helen ducked and Kevin covered her. The car swerved. They went up over a curb and crashed into a building. When the car came to a stop, Helen pushed Kevin off her to sit up and see Charlie slumped over the steering wheel.

"Charlie!" she shouted. She reached forward and felt for a pulse.

"What the fuck you think you're doing?" Kevin yelled, pulling her back down. "It's not safe for you to be sitting up right now."

"Fuck that! Charlie's dead." She struggled to free herself, but Kevin held her down. They heard another round of gunfire and Helen knew Kevin was right. They had to stay low.

She slumped under Kevin and waited until the screeching tires sounded and the shooters sped off.

"Those were Capone's men. I recognize them," Kevin said.

"Fuckers," Helen said.

They climbed out of the car. Helen bolted across the street to headquarters while Kevin and Jimmy carried Charlie's lifeless body.

Helen was in shock. She couldn't believe they'd taken Charlie. She also couldn't believe how close they'd come to getting her. She felt numb. She wanted to give up, to send up a white flag so no more of her men would die. The feeling didn't last long. Anger soon took hold and she vowed to even the score. She wanted to hit Moretti or close to him. This would take some planning.

They called Flander's to take away the body. Helen and Kevin drove to Charlie's house to tell his wife. Her anger grew as she held the woman and listened to the shrill shrieking as she wailed her grief.

Helen and Kevin went back to headquarters and grabbed the men who were there. They all went to the Golden Beaver for drinks. Partially to drown their sorrow and partially as a wake to celebrate the life of Charlie.

"Fuck me." Kevin captured Helen's attention and motioned toward the door. In walked Moretti with Maria and a handful of men.

"You've got a lot of fucking nerve," Helen said as he reached their table.

"What?"

"You asshole. Get the fuck out of my bar and take your whore and your goons with you."

Maria slapped Helen. Moretti stood his ground.

"I'd watch what you call her," he said.

"Get out of here," Helen repeated.

"What is your problem?" Moretti asked.

"As if you don't fucking know. You killed one of my men today. It's takes balls to show up at my place after that."

"I didn't do anything of the sort. I didn't even hear about it," Moretti said.

"Bullshit. You ordered that hit and one of my best men is dead. Now get the fuck out of my bar, or I won't be responsible for any actions of my men."

"I'll go," Moretti said. "But I swear I don't know what you're talking about. I'm sorry you lost a man today, Helen. But I had nothing to do with it."

He left with his entourage and Helen sat fuming. The nerve of the man to stand there and lie to her face. She downed her drink and then another. She needed to numb the pain of the day.

Her face still stung from Maria's slap. She acknowledged to herself that she'd gone too far. But she was livid as Maria had stood there, next to him, acting all smug and innocent. She'd chosen Moretti over Helen, and Helen had to accept that. But she didn't have to accept the bitch in her bar with that lying asshole.

She ordered another drink and walked back to her table.

"Can you believe that guy?" Kevin said.

"He's got balls the size of Texas," Helen said.

"You sure didn't make any points with Maria there."

"Fuck her."

Kevin just looked at her. She was pissed in all sorts of directions.

"What are we going to do about what they did today?" Kevin asked.

"They'll pay. Trust me."

❖

A month later, Helen still hadn't ordered the hit on Moretti, but she was biding her time, waiting for the prime opportunity. She wanted them completely unaware when it happened. She sat at her desk crunching numbers when Jimmy came rushing in.

"They hit Genna!"

"What? Bloody Angelo? Who hit him?"

"Some of Weiss's men. They followed him in his car. He lost control of it and wrapped it around a pole. Then they got out of the car and shot him. He's dead."

"That's fantastic! Good for them. Genna was a piece of shit."

Kevin poured the drinks in celebration. The atmosphere was more jubilant than it had been in weeks. They headed to the Beaver to keep the party going.

"So what are we gonna do about Moretti?" Kevin asked after a few drinks. "You didn't forget about him, did you?"

"How could I? We'll avenge Charlie's death. Don't you worry. Tonight, we're celebrating, though."

"I think we should hit Gattino's," Jimmy said.

"We can't hit Gattino's. We go there too often."

"But Moretti's always there," Kevin argued.

"He frequents other places, too. We'll hit him. I promise."

"Wouldn't it be great if we killed that son of a bitch?" Jimmy said.

"That's the plan," Helen said, the idea hitting her like a ton of bricks. "We need to take aim directly at him. We can't hit Big Al, so we'll aim for Moretti."

"Nice, boss." Kevin left to get another round.

"Do you mean that?" Jimmy asked. "Are you really gonna aim that high?"

"You'd better believe it." Helen realized she'd had a few drinks, but the idea grew on her. It would be so much nicer than just a random hit on his underlings. To actually take aim at Moretti would be an accomplishment to be proud of. She'd only trust her best men to the job. It was a shame Charlie was gone.

Kevin returned with the drinks.

"So when are we gonna do this?" he asked.

"We'll have to wait a little while longer," Helen said. "They'll be on alert after this hit on Genna. If the leader of the Genna family could be killed, Capone's men are going to be extra careful."

"Well, how long will we have to wait?" Kevin said.

"I don't know, Kevin. I'll know when the time is right though. And at that time, we'll kill the smug fucker."

"That's gonna be the happiest day in my life," Jimmy said.

"Mine, too," Helen agreed.

❖

Two weeks later, Helen called a meeting with her lieutenants.

"It's time to avenge Charlie's death," she said. "We're going to make it our mission to get Moretti. I want him dead."

"Where are we going to do this?" Kevin asked.

"Jimmy, you, William, and George gather about ten others and hit the Green Door. I've been there a couple times. Moretti's table is in the south corner. I want you to burst in, shoot up the place and make sure you hit Moretti. Get out of their fast. And be safe. I don't plan to lose another man."

"When is this going down?" Jimmy asked.

"Tonight. Say eleven o'clock. That should give them enough time to have had a few drinks and be a little slower when retaliating. I'm guessing their reflexes will be compromised. Still, it's critical you're alert. Don't be heroes. If you can't get

Moretti, get who you can. I don't want you leaving any men behind. Do I make myself clear?"

The men called their finest guys and had them come down to headquarters, where they finalized their plan. They'd barge through security and start shooting before the alarm could be sounded. They were to make it inside as far as they could so they could hit Moretti at his table. If Moretti wasn't there, they were to shoot as many people as they could. Either way, several of them would shoot up the booze behind the bar while the rest of them would gun for Moretti and his men.

They played poker to pass the time. Kevin and Helen left to pick up pizza for everyone.

"Boss, I'm really excited about tonight. It's a good thing they're finally going to get what's coming to them."

"I agree. I want Moretti dead more than you can imagine."

"Then you get the girl back, huh?"

Getting Maria back was something Helen only dared to dream of. It would be wonderful, to be sure.

"Eliminating Moretti is my priority, Kevin. I doubt Maria would want anything to do with me after I kill her man."

"What's her story anyway?"

"What do you mean?"

"I mean, she's with Moretti. Then she goes with you, then back to Moretti. Does she like men or women? Or both, maybe?"

"I think she likes women. But I think that scares her. The world expects her to be with a man. And God knows, she's been with enough of them."

"You don't really need someone that messed up, boss."

"Maybe not, but I really like her. She's different, Kevin. I can't explain it."

They returned with the pizzas and everyone dug in. Helen watched her men with pride. She was as excited as a kid at Christmas. She wished she could be part of the hit, but she knew it was too risky. Her job was to assign her men to do things. She was the brains of the organization. They'd be lost if anything happened to her.

Ten thirty arrived and the men left. Helen and Kevin poured themselves drinks and waited. They played cards with the other men who were hanging around headquarters. They tried to avoid looking at the clock every five minutes, but it wasn't easy.

Finally, the men came back, two of them nursing gunshot wounds.

"Get them to the hospital," she barked. Two of the guys who hadn't gone helped the men into their cars and left to drive them to the hospital.

"How did it go?" Helen asked Jimmy when the others were on their way.

"Excellent. We hit Moretti several times. He was on the floor when we left."

"We shot up their booze selection, too," William said. "I don't think we left a bottle unhit."

"Good job. How many others did you get?"

"We shot a lot of people. The place was jumpin'," George said. "A few of us sprayed the crowd while the rest of them went after Moretti and William's guys hit the bar area."

"You guys did good," Helen said. "Kevin, pour these men some drinks."

Helen left the party to check on the men at the hospital. Both were fine, so she paid their bills and followed them back to headquarters. The celebration lasted late into the night. Helen felt great as she finally left to go home for few hours of sleep. She didn't know if Moretti had made it or not, but she could only hope he was gone. It was time for her to be able to live her life without that man always ruining it.

Chapter Nineteen

"Any news on Moretti?" Helen asked Kevin when he arrived at headquarters late the following morning.

"He's fine," Kevin said. "He got hit a couple times, but nothing serious. He was in and out of the hospital last night."

"Shit," Helen said. Not only was he alive, but he was going to be one pissed adversary.

"No one said anything about hitting Maria, did they?" Kevin asked.

"No."

"I guess that's good for you."

"I guess. I don't really care," Helen said.

"Says you."

"So I wonder when Moretti will retaliate," Helen said, nauseous that her archenemy was still alive.

"Hard to say. Could be anytime, though."

"Yeah. We'll just keep vigilant and watch everyone around us at all times."

They went about their business as usual the next couple of weeks and everything went smoothly. There were no hits on them and Helen started to relax a little.

She met Kevin at Mickey's one morning and Kevin had some news for her.

"Another member of the Genna family is dead," he said.

"Who? What happened?"

"Mike Genna was riding with some of his men when they got in a shootout with the cops. Two cops were killed, as well as Genna."

"That leaves only Tony, right? He's the last of the Gennas."

"He is and no one knows where he is. Rumor has it Scalise and Anselmi of the Genna gang have switched over to working for Big Al. I'm sure they're not the only ones."

"Shit. The Gennas never gunned for us. And Al doesn't need to get any bigger. I don't like thinking of Genna's men working for him."

"Could be a rumor, boss, but I heard it from a pretty reliable source."

"I never doubt your sources, Kevin."

"We've got money waiting. Let's get back to collecting," Helen said.

They said their good-byes to Mickey, and Kevin walked outside to make sure the coast was clear.

Helen heard the sound of gunfire and watched Kevin hit the ground.

"Call an ambulance!" Helen told Mickey. She wanted to rush out to check on Kevin, but knew that could be suicide. She waited until she heard the sirens, followed by the squeal of tires. Thinking she was safe, she raced out and met the ambulance. She caught sight of one of the men looking back from the car racing away. He was Moretti's man. Helen fumed.

"Kevin!" she screamed, but he didn't respond. Mickey was right behind her, his face pale in fear and worry.

"Kevin?" He knelt and took Kevin's head in his lap.

The ambulance driver had to push Mickey out of the way to get Kevin on a gurney.

"We'll take him to Sacred Heart," he told Helen.

Helen followed the ambulance and paced in the waiting room while Kevin was in surgery. Mickey was there as well, sitting with his head in his hands.

"We came as soon as we heard." Jimmy came in, followed by several men. "How is he?"

"We don't know anything yet," Helen said.

They waited in silence until the doctor came in, grim faced.

"We've done all we can do. It doesn't look good."

"When can we see him?" Helen asked.

"He's in recovery. He'll be in his room in a few hours."

"What should we do, boss?" Jimmy asked after the doctor left.

"Go on home. I'll stay with Kevin."

"You want us to go after someone?"

Helen was numb. Kevin was at death's doorstep. As much as she knew someone should pay for this, she wasn't able to formulate a plan.

"Give me some time," she said. "I can't think right now."

"Okay. Well, we'll leave you here, but we'll be back to check on him. He's gonna be okay. He's a survivor."

Helen nodded. She wanted to believe that, but the doctor's words scared her.

Kevin was moved to a room and Helen sat at his bedside. Others came to visit, but Helen stayed put. Kevin looked so peaceful sleeping. Helen wondered what was going through his mind, if anything. She was happy to see him stress free, but wished more than anything that he'd wake up.

Mickey came by every day to check on Kevin. Helen left during those times to give them some privacy. She never left the hospital, though.

"Why don't you go home for a break?" Jimmy asked on the third day of her vigil. "I'll stay with him and I'll call you if there's any change."

"Thanks, but my place is with him. He'd do the same thing for me. I want to be here when he wakes up."

She spent the hours casting her memory back to their days coming up on the streets. She remembered Kevin standing up for her on more than one occasion. Helen had always been the brains and usually kept them out of trouble, but there were a couple of times that she'd talked them into a corner and Kevin had come out swinging. She always knew she was safe as long as Kevin was around.

Helen woke from a quick doze on the fifth day and looked at the sleeping form of her friend of all those years. She felt so hopeless, wishing there was something she could do for him.

Suddenly, Kevin's eyes fluttered open.

"Kevin!" she called out. She grabbed his hand and held it tightly. "Kevin, you're awake!"

His eyes closed again, and he exhaled, then lay silent.

"Kevin? Kevin!" Helen collapsed over his still form. "Kevin, no you don't. You're not gonna die. Not on my watch."

He didn't respond, and she knew it was useless. Her right-hand man was gone.

❖

The cemetery was filled with men who had come to pay their final respects to Kevin Donegal. Helen was surrounded, her men determined that nothing would happen to her. She threw dirt on the coffin as it was lowered into the ground. She fought the tears that threatened. She was crushed but knew better than to show any weakness in public.

She climbed into the backseat of Jimmy's car and waited for the others to pile in. They drove back to headquarters in silence. Helen swallowed hard when they arrived. It wasn't the same without Kevin's constant presence.

Jimmy poured her a drink, which she gladly accepted. She knew she had to get it together soon, as her men were looking to her for leadership. She could grieve on her own time, but for now, they needed her.

"We should go to the Beaver," Jimmy suggested.

"We'll get there," Helen said. "I need some time first."

She knew she needed to go on, but the desire to crawl into a hole was overwhelming. She thought about letting Jimmy run things for a while, but she knew that wouldn't work. What would she do if she wasn't running the gang? She'd sit around and be miserable. She needed to get her head back into the business to occupy her mind. And she needed to get even with Moretti for killing Kevin.

The men were getting restless, so Helen pulled herself together.

"Let's go to the Beaver. Kevin needs a proper send off."

Helen wanted to drive, but her men wouldn't hear of it. She agreed with them. She needed constant protection. So she climbed into Jimmy's car once more.

They had the place to themselves for several hours, during which many of the men went upstairs to spend some time with the girls. Helen stayed at her table, drinking more than she should, but not caring. She wasn't about to get drunk, but it felt good to have a little buzz. She needed to dull the sharp edge of pain that had become a constant in her life.

Slowly but surely, the place livened up. Soon, the atmosphere was raucous, with the band playing and people dancing and drinking.

Helen was lost in thought and was surprised when her men jumped to their feet. She followed their gazes to the door and felt like she'd been punched in her gut when she saw Maria walk in. She stayed seated as Maria crossed to her table.

"What do you want?" Helen asked.

"I heard about Kevin."

"I'm sure you did."

"Helen, I'm very sorry. Really, I am."

"So am I," Helen said.

"May I sit down?" Maria asked.

Helen shrugged.

Maria sat next to her and wrung her hands. Helen felt the tension between them and could barely remember that they'd been lovers.

"Where's Moretti?" Helen asked.

"I don't know."

"I hope you're happy with him."

"I'm not. I left him," Maria said.

"You what?"

"I said I left him. When I heard about Kevin, I left Franco. I can't be with him."

"But you chose him over me. Why would Kevin's death change your mind?"

"I never stopped caring about you, Helen."

"Spare me."

"This isn't easy for me," Maria said.

"Let me make it easy for you. Get out of here. Leave and don't come back."

Maria stood, a lone tear streaming down her cheek.

"I can't change your mind?"

"Why are you crying?"

"Helen, I'm telling you I want another chance with you."

"Now isn't a good time for me," Helen said.

"That's fine." Maria sat back down. "I don't need an answer now. I just want you to know I'm here for you."

"You left Moretti for killing someone. How many people has he killed before? Why Kevin?"

"Because I know how close you and Kevin were. And I realized that Franco'd stop at nothing to kill you. I'm sure you know that. When Kevin was killed, it really hit home. And I can't be with him. I mean, I knew you were enemies, but it didn't connect. Even with all the shootings. But now I see that you won't stop until one of you is dead. I can't choose him over you."

Helen listened to Maria and willed herself to believe her. Wasn't this what she wanted? To have Maria leave Moretti and come back to her? Why wasn't she able to appreciate it? She should be excited, bouncing up and down and welcoming Maria back with open arms. Still, she felt numb.

"I guess I'm not very good company tonight," she said lamely. "I don't even know what to say."

Maria stood again.

"I understand. You don't have to say anything. When you're able to think about something besides Kevin, whenever that is, please think about what I said. You have my number. I'm only a phone call away."

Chapter Twenty

"I want someone tailing Moretti at all times," Helen told her men. "I don't want him pissing without me knowing about it."

"Who's gonna do that?" Jimmy asked.

"Divvy it up among all of you. Figure it out. But I don't want him ever out of our sight. I'm not going to quit 'til he's dead. Am I making myself clear?"

"You got it."

"And if you see an opening, for God's sake, take it."

Helen settled in to work on the ledgers, which she'd neglected for several weeks. It was nice to be back. She felt almost normal. She kept expecting to see Kevin every time she turned around, but the numbness was receding, anger and hatred taking its place.

She was determined that Moretti would pay for Kevin's death. When all the men except the faction assigned to guard her cleared out to make the rounds, she focused on the numbers for about an hour until thoughts of Maria floated through her mind. She hadn't called her, hadn't even thought about her since that night at the Beaver.

She wondered how serious Maria had been. Sure, she didn't want to be with Moretti anymore, but would she really want to be with Helen? Was it the killing and violence that Maria despised or was she truly choosing Helen over Moretti?

She made herself finish entering numbers, happy with the way the books were looking. Money was rolling in. Businesses were prospering, although not in the neighborhood around Mickey's. Helen made a mental note to swing by Mickey's to see how he was doing. She hadn't seen him since the funeral. She wondered yet again about the relationship between him and Kevin. She was sad for Kevin if he had truly been in love, but lived his life hiding it.

The thought brought her back to Maria. Try as she might, she couldn't keep her mind off her. She finally gave up and called her.

For the first time in a long time, Maria took her call.

"Hello, Helen. Thank you for calling."

"I felt I owed it to you. It's the least I could do."

"Well, that's not promising."

"I'm sorry I wasn't better company the other night."

"You already apologized for that," Maria said.

"I don't know what to say. I'm not sure why I called," Helen said.

"I don't know either, but I'm glad you did."

"Can I take you to lunch?"

"I'd like that."

"Good. I'll be there at noon. But I won't be alone."

"Fair enough. I'll be ready."

Helen arrived at exactly noon. She sent up a man to Maria's door as she sat in the car, on edge. Her other men who followed them were out of their car, looking everywhere. Helen's man and Maria returned to the car and Maria sat in the backseat with Helen. The other men got in their car and the entourage drove off.

Helen breathed a little easier as they reached the West Side and were surrounded by friendly sights. They drove to Donovan's for lunch. The men scattered throughout the restaurant, determined to keep their eyes open for anyone suspicious. Helen and Maria sat quietly at their own table.

"It's so strange to have you surrounded by all these men," Maria said.

"It's necessary. I doubt Moretti will stop with Kevin."

"I'm so sorry about that," Maria said.

"So explain to me again why you left Moretti," Helen said.

"I told you. If one of you is going to die, I'd rather it not be you. So I can't be with him knowing that's his goal."

"To be clear, then, is it the fact that he's gunning for me the problem? Or is it all the killing in general?"

"I don't like killing, Helen. But I've been involved with gangs since I was a kid. It's part of the life. I know this. I don't like that Moretti wants you dead."

Helen ordered their lunches and wine. It was almost like before. Almost. Yet the pain from being dumped was still there. She wanted their relationship back, but she didn't want to be hurt again.

"You understand why I hesitate to simply embrace you and take you back, don't you?"

"Of course," Maria said. "But please understand. I really thought you were using me. That hurt."

"I was keeping you safe. I wanted to make sure you weren't at the gambling hall that night," Helen said.

"I believe you now. But I didn't then. I thought you just needed an alibi."

"But what about all the other times we were together? What did you think of those times?"

"I thought you were just setting me up. I felt like I knew what I was getting with Moretti. So I chose him. But my heart lies with you. I realize this now."

"Well, I'm glad you came to your senses."

"I do hope you'll give me another chance, Helen."

"I'm here, aren't I?" Helen knew she sounded cold, but her heart was too tender to just offer it up again. "We can go out, see if we still fit. We'll take it slow."

Their conversation was interrupted when the waiter brought their food.

"I'd like that." Maria reached across the table and took Helen's hand.

Helen's heart skipped a beat. She'd missed Maria's touch. It was soft and caring, and as much as she wished she could deny it, it felt good. She squeezed back.

"We can take it as slow as you need to," Maria said.

"Thank you for understanding. My heart's a little raw right now. I can't take much more loss."

"I'm not going to hurt you again. I promise."

"I want to believe you. I do. It's just not easy."

Helen took her hand back and they started on their lunches.

"So when did you call it off with Moretti?" Helen asked.

"Two days before I last saw you."

"How'd he take it?"

"Not well. He called me some choice names and told me I'd never amount to anything without him."

"What a schmuck. You're much better off without him."

"I think so. He was so angry at me. I was scared. I still am, a little."

"He'd better not try to hurt you."

"Part of me thinks I'm not worth it to him, but part of me thinks I made him look like a dunce and he'll want to get back at me."

"I'd assign one of my guys to you, but I don't want any of my men spending that much time in the South. You're welcome to stay with me."

"What happened to taking it slow?"

"We can still take it slow. Trust me."

"Are you sure you don't mind? I'd feel safer."

"Sure. Just know I'm seldom alone," Helen said.

"I can understand that. I'm sure you're a target, now more than ever."

"I'll send some men over after lunch to pack up some things."

"Thank you, Helen."

"You're welcome."

❖

Helen sent four of her men with instructions not to let Maria out of their sight unless Helen was with her. Her squadron drove her back to headquarters. She found Jimmy there with several other men.

"What are you guys doing?" she asked.

"We just finished our takes. You want me to make rounds with you?" Jimmy said.

Helen realized she'd eventually have to introduce someone else with her when she made her collections, but it was too soon. Or so it felt. The reality was, now was as good a time as any. It wasn't safe for her to go alone, and Jimmy was proving himself in the gang.

• 183 •

"Sure. Let's go pick up some cash." She pointed to two young guns, Ralphie and Hank. "One of you drive. The other ride shotgun. Let's go."

"I could have driven, boss," Jimmy said when they were in the car.

"No. You sit back here with me. Hank will keep me safe from his place. You'll keep me safe from there. That's how I want it."

"You got it."

Jimmy met all the people on Helen's route. No one asked any questions. They just accepted that he was a new guy. When they finally got to Mickey's, Helen stopped out front.

"You guys hang out here. I'll go in there alone."

"You sure? That doesn't seem safe."

"I'm sure," Helen said, knowing it would kill Mickey to see someone in Kevin's place.

She walked in and was greeted with a bear hug. Mickey held her for a full minute before pulling away.

"Good to see you, Helen. Will you be having lunch today?"

"No. I'm just here to see how business is."

"Oh, sure." Mickey reached behind the register and pulled out a thick white envelope. "Business has been booming."

"Good. How are you, Mickey?"

"I have my good days. I have my bad days. Work keeps me busy, and for this, I'm grateful. Any news on the asshole who did it?"

"Don't worry. I'm having him watched closely."

"I hope you get the bastard," Mickey said.

"We will, Mickey. I give you my word."

The group headed back to headquarters, and Helen got to work splitting the money up among the lieutenants for them to share with their men. She made her entries in the ledger, handed out the money, and put the remainder in the safe. She made a mental note to give Jimmy the combination. Kevin had been the only one besides herself who knew it.

Thoughts of Kevin were with her at all times still. She missed him terribly. Jimmy was doing his best to step up, but he wasn't Kevin. Jimmy had moved to Chicago several years earlier and met up with Kevin in a bar. Kevin had immediately brought him to Helen, telling her he'd worked for the Beacon Hill boys in Boston.

Helen welcomed him and hadn't been disappointed. He was always bringing more money and new ideas. He was the one who'd suggested they start selling hashish as well as marijuana at the Beaver and Lucky's. He was smart and willing. Two traits Helen admired and needed.

"Shall we go to the Beaver?" He broke through her thoughts.

"Sure. Give me a minute."

She called her apartment. Maria answered.

"Hi, Maria. Get the guys to bring you to the Beaver."

"Do I have to take orders from you now?"

"I'm sorry. Maria, would you like to go to the Beaver with us?" Helen rolled her eyes on her end of the phone.

"I'd like that. Thanks."

"Great. Have the guys bring you. We'll see you there in a few."

Chapter Twenty-one

Helen arrived with her men a good half hour before Maria and her contingent. Maria looked beautiful in a black dress with a black hat that came almost to her eyes. Helen's breath caught at the sight of her. She was proud that this woman wanted her. She was thrilled Maria had chosen her over Moretti.

"You look swell." Helen kissed her cheek.

"Thank you." Maria sat next to her and took her hand.

They listened to a few songs before Maria said, "Are you going to ask me to dance?"

Helen laughed, more relaxed than she had been in weeks. "Would you like to dance?"

"No, thanks," Maria said, then laughed. "I'm teasing. I'd love to dance with you."

They danced some fast songs until the band slowed it down for them. Maria moved into Helen's arms. They moved together as one.

"This is just like old times, huh?" Maria said.

"It's nice," Helen said.

Maria moved against her.

"So how slow are we taking things?"

"That's a very good question," Helen whispered in her ear.

The dance ended and they walked back to the table and sat down. Jimmy went to the bar to get drinks for them. He'd only just gotten back when the door burst open and gunshots filled the speakeasy.

Helen fell on Maria and Jimmy fell on her. They lay like that for what seemed like hours, but was really a matter of minutes. The gunshots ended and the gang of men left as quickly as they'd come in.

Slowly, patrons got up off the floor and dusted themselves off. Jimmy helped Helen and Maria to their feet. They looked around. Some of their men had been hit, but everyone else seemed fine.

"Get these men to the hospital," Helen cried.

There was a flurry of activity as men were helped out of the bar and into cars. No one seemed seriously injured, but the bullets had done their damage.

"How are we looking?" Helen asked Jimmy as she looked around.

"Looks like the bar itself was shot up, but the only people hit were ours. I'd say those men knew exactly where to aim, boss. You're lucky you're alive."

"Shit!"

Maria was shaking. Helen wrapped her coat around her.

"You need to get us home. Then get to the bottom of the shooting. I want answers when I see you in the morning."

They drove home in silence, Jimmy driving Helen and Maria while the other cars followed. The men assigned to them would sleep at Helen's apartment as well. Except Jimmy. He and his handpicked men would be looking into the shooting.

Helen helped Maria inside and held her close as she cried. "You see what my life is like? You sure you want to be with me?"

"I'm just sorry. I feel like I brought this on you."

"Did you see the shooters?" Helen asked. "Were they Moretti's men?"

Maria shook her head.

"No, as in they weren't his men?"

"No. I mean I didn't see them. I'm sorry."

"Hush, now. It's okay. Jimmy'll find out who it was and we'll get even with them. For now, let's get you to bed."

She led Maria to her room and left while she undressed for bed.

"Where are you sleeping?" Maria asked when Helen came back in.

"I'm afraid I'll have to sleep in here. We barely have enough room for the men as it is. But don't worry. I have no intention of doing anything but sleeping."

"Will you at least hold me?" Maria asked.

"I could do that." Helen slid into bed and wrapped her arms around Maria, pulling her close. She could feel the tension slowly draining out of her. Helen knew she probably wouldn't sleep much, but hoped at least Maria would be able to get some rest.

❖

"What did you find out?" Helen asked Jimmy as soon as he arrived to pick her up the next morning.

"They were definitely Moretti's people," Jimmy said. "Boss, we've got to do something about them."

"What do we know about Moretti? No one's seen him open enough for a clear shot?"

"Not yet, Helen. We're still tailing him. He's not a stupid man, though. He's lost our tail several times so far."

"I expected nothing less. Still, I want us to stay on him as best we can."

"So what's our next move?"

"First thing I want to do is make sure there's booze at the Beaver. I want that place open for business tonight."

"I'll check the basement, but I'm fairly certain we just got a large shipment."

"Take some men over there and check to be sure. And clean it up. I want as little evidence of last night as possible. You got that?"

"Got it." He called some men to meet him there. "Are you going to be okay here?" he asked before he left.

"I'll be fine. I've got these men." She waved at the contingent she'd assigned to herself.

"Don't go anywhere without them," he cautioned.

"I'm the one who gives the orders, Jimmy. But don't worry. I'm not making a move unless I'm covered."

"Good. We've lost too many people lately. You're too valuable to add to that list."

"Thank you, Jimmy. Now go get some work done."

After Jimmy was gone, Helen set to work trying to figure out how best to lure Moretti away from his goons long enough to kill him. Her first thought was to use Maria, but she wasn't about to risk her life. Moretti would have to be caught some other way.

The thought of Maria made Helen miss her. It had been nice to hold her the night before, although the circumstances weren't the greatest. Helen was so glad to have her back, but worried that she'd lose her again. She didn't want to think about that depth of pain again. She'd had enough loss in her life. Still, she should make the most of their time together. She wanted to see her, to spend time with her.

She called her apartment.

"Hello?" Maria answered.

"Hey, there. What are you doing?"

"I just got out of the tub. What are you doing?"

"Thinking about taking you to lunch."

"That would be great," Maria said. "I'd like that very much."

"Great. Have the boys drive you to Bulger's. We'll have lunch."

"What time? It'll take me some time to get ready."

"We'll meet in an hour," Helen said.

She arrived at Bulger's before Maria and sat at her usual table while her men took seats at the tables around her. She hated the lack of privacy, but it was a small price to pay to stay alive. She shuddered to think what could happen if she was ever caught alone by Moretti's men.

Maria walked in wearing a red dress with a black sash around her waist. Or the waist of her dress, rather. It hung closer to her hips. Helen again thought back to the time women wore clothes that accentuated, rather than downplayed their figures. Still, Maria looked beautiful. The charcoal around her eyes was a perfect accent to the brown pools Helen enjoyed so much.

Helen stood and crossed the room to greet her. She took her hands and kissed her cheek.

"You look swell," she said.

"Thanks, so do you."

"I'm not even wearing a jacket," Helen protested.

"You look great even in your shirtsleeves."

Helen held Maria's chair for her before sitting down again.

"How has your day been?" Maria asked.

"It's been peachy."

"Seriously?"

"The guys are working to get the Beaver opened tonight. That's about all that's going on." Helen contemplated telling her that she'd spent a good portion of the morning trying to come up with a way to hit Moretti, but opted against it.

"Did you find out who was behind last night?"

"We did." Helen took a sip of wine.

"Who was it?"

"You know I don't like talking about work."

"Who was it?" Maria asked again.

"It was Moretti's men."

"That bastard. Didn't Jimmy say that was a direct attempt at you?"

"That's what he said."

"What are you going to do about Franco?"

"What do you think I should do?" Helen asked.

"Why are you asking me? Are you making fun of me?"

"No, doll. I'm curious what you think I should do about the guy."

"I don't know. But I'm surprised you let him bully you like he does."

"Ouch." Helen laughed at Maria's spunk.

"Well, I don't know how else to say it," Maria said.

"I don't exactly *let* him bully me. He's just pissed at me and making sure I know."

"By trying to kill you."

"I'll admit, if he up and moved away I wouldn't shed a tear."

"But that ain't gonna happen."

"I know, doll. He's got it good."

"He's a made man in Capone's gang. He's got it *real* good."

"Not exactly the perfect conversation for a meal," Helen said as their meals were delivered.

"I'm sorry. I don't mean to upset you," Maria said when the waiter left.

"You didn't. The guy just gets my goat. I need to get even with him."

"Are you gonna kill him?" Maria asked.

Helen was shocked at Maria's matter-of-fact question. She took a sip of wine and weighed her options.

"What if I did? How would you feel?"

Maria was silent for a moment.

"I don't know how else to say this," she finally said.

"Just say it."

"I'd dance on the bastard's grave."

Helen choked.

"Well, you told me to say what I was thinking," Maria said.

"I did." Helen laughed. "I just thought you might tell me how much you'd miss him or something like that."

"Miss him? The guy's a jerk. I regret the time I spent with him. I'm so sorry I chose him over you before."

"So am I."

"I'll never make that mistake again."

"You won't, huh?"

"I promise."

"Well, hopefully we'll get him taken care of and that won't be an option."

"No joke? That would be great."

"Well, it's not something I want you to worry your head over."

"I can tell you where he stays most of the time. He's like you. He's got apartments all over town, but I know his main lair. You could get him there."

Helen felt like it was Christmas, and she'd gotten her favorite toy.

"You'd do that?"

"Of course. Why wouldn't I?"

Helen felt the last vestiges of her reservations melt away. Maria was serious about being her dame. She jumped out of her seat and moved across the table to kiss Maria. She kissed her with all the passion she'd been denying. When the kiss ended, she was breathing heavily.

"Wow, that made me dizzy," Maria whispered against her mouth.

"Take us back to the apartment," she ordered the men.

Chapter Twenty-two

When they returned to the apartment, Helen told the men to relax for a while before leading Maria into the bedroom.

She pulled her into her arms as soon as the door closed behind them. She held her tightly, reveling in the feel of their bodies together.

"I've missed you," Helen whispered.

"I've missed you, too," Maria said.

Helen kissed her cheek and neck, determined to go slowly and not rush this important moment. Maria shuddered in her arms when she kissed where her neck met her shoulder. Helen knew she was in for a wonderful afternoon.

She cupped Maria's face and traced her cheeks with her thumbs. Her skin was so soft and smooth. She dragged a thumb across her lips before lowering her mouth to taste her.

When their lips met, Helen felt the earth tilt. She struggled to stay upright as the kiss intensified. Dizzy with need, she finally collapsed onto the bed, pulling Maria with her.

They continued to kiss, their tongues dancing playfully over each other. Each pass of Maria's tongue fanned the flame threatening to consume Helen. Soon Maria was whimpering as she pressed into her.

Helen ran her hands over Maria's body, frustrated by the barrier of clothing separating them. She fumbled with the sash Maria wore, finally untying it. She broke the kiss and lay breathing heavily under Maria.

"We need to get out of these clothes," she said.

Maria sat up and pulled her dress over her head.

"Is this better?" she asked.

"Much."

Helen struggled out of her own clothes while Maria removed her undergarments.

Finally, they were both naked.

"My God, you're beautiful," Helen said.

"You're not so bad yourself," Maria said, running her hands over Helen's chest.

"I mean it," Helen said. "You take my breath away. I don't think I'll ever get enough of you."

She rolled over so they lay side by side. She skimmed her hand over Maria's body, lightly tracing the length of her. She felt her skin ripple at the touch. She brought a hand to rest on one of her breasts and teased it with more gentle touches before taking the nipple between her finger and thumb.

Maria drew in her breath. Helen held her like that, barely applying any pressure, just enjoying the feel of the hard nub. She pinched harder and Maria cried out from the pleasure it created.

Helen kissed her again, deeply and passionately as she gently twisted the nipple. She moved her hand to the other breast and did the same thing. She kissed down her neck and chest and put her mouth where her hand was.

She licked at the nipple, long slow laps and short, deliberate strokes. She licked her areola and down to the base of her breast, pausing to suck on the tender skin.

She ran her hand down Maria's belly and slowly caressed first one inner thigh, then the other.

"Please, Helen," Maria said. "Please touch me."

Helen needed no further prodding. She let her hand find Maria's center and was greeted with Maria's hips arching into her. She rubbed light circles around her clit, urging her onward toward their goal. She placed her fingers on her clit and pressed into her until she needed more. She slipped her fingers deep inside Maria's satin softness. She felt her close around her. Helen twisted her hand and pulled out slightly, then twisted again as she moved back inside.

Maria spread her legs wider and Helen went deeper. She caressed the softness that met her fingers deep in the recesses of Maria. Each stroke had Maria moving against her faster, moving her hips around and around to guide Helen toward the spots that needed to be touched.

Helen finally rubbed the special place that she knew would send Maria over the edge. She rubbed it gently, then harder, until she felt Maria clench around her as she catapulted her into the climax she so desperately craved.

When she felt the spasms subside, she stroked the spot again and was rewarded by Maria seizing up before relaxing into yet another orgasm.

Helen held Maria after, kissing her softly.

"There's something I should tell you," she said.

"What is it?"

"It's fairly serious and I'm not really sure how to say it."

"You're scaring me, Helen."

"Oh, no! It's nothing bad. At least I don't think it is."
"Tell me."
Helen rolled over so she was looking into Maria's eyes.
"Maria..."
"Yes?"
"I could see myself falling in love with you."
"You could, huh?"
"I could." She kissed her again.
"I could like that," Maria said when the kiss ended.
"Good."

Maria moved on top of Helen and kissed her. She kissed down her cheek to her chest and played with her nipples while she brought her knee up against her.

Helen pressed into her leg and tangled her hands in Maria's hair, holding her head in place while her sucking caused electrical currents to flow to the nerve center between her legs. She rubbed against Maria's knee, coating it as her excitement grew.

Maria let loose of the nipple in her mouth and kissed down Helen's taut belly until she was kneeling between her legs. She dipped her head and licked along every inch of Helen, who squirmed at the feelings she was creating. Helen gasped as she felt Maria's tongue inside her, lapping at her, touching her sensitive spots. She placed her hand on the back of Maria's head as she found her sensitive clit and licked at it fervently.

Helen felt myriad sensations washing over her as Maria ravished her. Her head grew light as she felt the heat balling up in her center. All her focus was on her clit and the pit in her stomach, both of which grew larger by the second. When she could take no more, she allowed herself to let go and felt the heat course through her veins as the powerful climax racked her body.

"Baby, you need to stop," she said, her clit tender after the orgasm.

"Do I have to?" Maria asked.

"Yes. I can't take any more."

Maria kissed back up Helen's body and curled into her. Helen held her tight against her as they drifted off in a sated sleep.

Helen woke as Maria stirred and checked the clock on the bedside table. They'd been asleep for an hour.

"I need to get back to the office, doll," Helen said.

"Oh, do you have to?" Maria pouted.

Helen took Maria's lower lip between hers and sucked on it.

"I love your lips," she said.

"I love yours."

"That works well."

"Do you really have to go?"

"I do. I've got business to take care of." Helen climbed out of bed and got dressed.

"Did you want me to give you Franco's address?"

"You know it, doll."

"It's over on State Street. Two blocks south of Wabash. The building is called The Haven."

"I know the area. That's right by one of Capone's headquarters. This could be dangerous."

"Please be careful, Helen."

"I will."

❖

Helen was escorted back to the barbershop and found Jimmy and several others there.

"What's the news on Moretti?" she asked.

"He lost us again," Jimmy said.

"Damn. Well, we know where he lives now. Or one of the places. It's dangerous, but I want us to post some guys at his place."

"Where's the place?" Jimmy asked.

"Just south of Wabash on State."

"Shit! That's right in the middle of their gangland."

"I know. But I want him dead. I'm tired of him shooting us up. And last night was a direct hit on me. In our territory. I want to return the favor."

"So you just want us to sit there like ducks on a pond and wait for them to take us out?"

"No. I think I want a couple of the guys he won't know to rent apartments in the building."

"But anybody he won't know would be pretty wet. You sure you want to trust them with an assignment like this?"

"Who else? It can't be you or me or anyone they'd recognize. Choose some young bloods you trust. Bring them back here. I want to make sure they can handle this."

"But what if they get in there?" Jimmy said. "What if they do? Then they hit Moretti and they'll be dead before they can get out of there."

"Not if they're smart. Smart and fast. That's the only way they'll survive."

"Isn't there a way we can have more of us there?"

"Sure. I've got it. After they've been there a while, they can throw a party. We'll all go and we can all take out Moretti."

"I like the sound of that, boss."

"Good. So go get some men."

Jimmy returned a few hours later with two young men.

"Clyde and Leonard!" Helen cried when she saw the two men. "Excellent choices."

"What's goin' on?" Clyde asked.

"Jimmy didn't tell us nothin'," Leonard said.

"You guys know where The Haven apartment building is over on State Street?"

"Sure," Clyde said. "That's over by the Four Deuces. I know it."

"I want each of you to rent an apartment there. You've got to lay low and keep to yourselves, got it?"

"Sure," Leonard said. "But why?"

"That's where Moretti stays mostly. I want you two to watch him like a hawk. I want to know his schedule better than he does. You'll come back here daily to report in. But be sly about it. Make sure you're not followed. If you are, do *not* come anywhere near here. Your covers can't be blown."

"No shit. They'd kill us," Clyde said.

"In a heartbeat," Helen agreed.

"How long we gotta live there for?" Leonard asked.

"As long as it takes. I want him gone as soon as possible, but it's got to be perfectly planned. This is a lot of responsibility. If either of you don't want to do this, just say so."

"I'm in," Clyde said.

"Me, too," Leonard said.

"Good." Helen was pleased. "Let's see. Clyde, you're new in town. Just got in from Omaha."

"Omaha?" Clyde balked.

"You in or should I find someone else?"

"Fine. I'm from Omaha."

"You sell shoes. You work at Monroe's."

"Leonard, you just moved here from Duluth. You're looking for work."

"Can you guys remember that?"

"Sure thing."

"Good. Your lives depend on it."

Helen gave them money and sent them off to The Haven. She felt good about her plan. Now she had nothing to do but wait.

Chapter Twenty-three

It was hot and muggy in the apartment that Helen shared with Maria. July had been one of the hottest months on record, and August was shaping up to be more of the same. Helen lay in bed with Maria, trying to convince herself to get up and get to work when all she wanted to do was make love to Maria again.

They'd been watching Moretti for a while and were getting a good feel for his habits. She just needed a little more time and she'd be ready to take him out. She knew she should be at headquarters with her men, but Maria was so inviting.

"I need to hit the shower." Helen rolled over and got out of bed. "Care to join me?"

"I could use a shower."

They walked to the bathroom hand in hand. Helen held the door open and admired Maria as she stepped into the shower. She watched the water cascade over her body and longed to trace the rivulets herself.

Helen walked in behind Maria and wrapped her arms around her and pressed into her back. She ran her hands over Maria's breasts and down her belly. She brought her hands to her ass and lightly squeezed it. She kissed her shoulder and licked off the water droplets shimmering on her skin.

She pressed Maria against the wall and spread her legs with her knee. She slipped her hand between her legs and grinned at the slickness that waited for her. She reveled in the feeling, dragging her fingers along the whole area.

Maria spread her legs wider and Helen eased her hand further and rubbed her fingers over her clit. She pulled back and dipped her fingers inside. She moved them deep inside, caressing her walls as she did. She ran her fingertips over the softness she met, becoming more aroused by the moment.

She pressed her breasts against Maria's back, needing the pressure against her nipples. Maria moved against her, pulling her deeper. Helen continued moving inside her, almost at the point of bursting herself.

Maria froze as she finally achieved her release. She relaxed against Helen, who kept her fingers buried and coaxed another orgasm out of her.

Maria turned and kissed Helen hard on her mouth. Helen held tightly to Maria's lithe body, feeling every inch against her. She drew her breath as Maria nibbled her neck. The water washed over them as Maria took first one nipple then the other in her mouth. Helen felt her legs buckle at the sensations Maria was creating.

Helen leaned against the wall to brace herself as Maria moved her mouth lower, marking a trail down her belly with her tongue. Maria dropped to a knee and buried her face between Helen's legs. Her tongue flicked at Helen's clit, causing her nipples to tighten even further.

Maria pried her legs apart and lapped at the warm opening she found there. She delved her tongue deep inside, licking voraciously as she did.

Helen placed her hand on the back of Maria's head, pressing her into her. Maria moved her mouth back to Helen's clit and drew it between her lips. She ran her tongue over the hardened morsel and Helen felt the world tilt on its axis. She closed her eyes and focused on Maria's tongue and the way it was making her feel. Her mind went blank as the first waves of the climax approached.

Maria kept working her tongue, and soon Helen was engulfed in a massive orgasm that rocked her to her core.

When she was steady again, Helen soaped up her hands and ran them all over Maria's body, not stopping until Maria came again. Maria returned the favor, and they regained their bearings as they rinsed off.

They toweled each other off and Maria climbed back in bed.

"Doll, I wish I could stay, but I've got to get to work."

"I know, but I wanted you to have something to think about all day."

"I think about you all day anyway, Maria."

"Aw, baby. You say the sweetest things."

❖

Helen got to headquarters, where Jimmy informed her she'd just missed Clyde.

"Moretti got home around three again this morning," Jimmy said.

"That seems to be the pattern. We need to plan our attack."

"So when are we going to hit? Are we still going to do the party?"

"We're going to have the party to end all parties. Moretti's finally going to pay the piper."

"When, boss?"

"Let's plan on it for next week. You get the word out. I want at least twenty of us there. We're going to have to hit his goons, too, you know."

"Are you sure you want to do this? I mean, I know he's been gunning for you, but what happens when he's gone? Capone won't rest 'til you're dead if you kill one of his right-hand men."

"I've got a week to figure that out."

"You sure you want to wait a week? You might be hit by then."

"I'm not going to be hit. I'll be laying so low, they'll never find me. It's work and home for me, Jimmy. And it's not going to be a whole week. We'll hit him Monday night. We'll gather at eleven and wait 'til he gets home. He won't see it coming."

❖

Helen was home with Maria all afternoon the following Monday. She'd spent most of the morning at the bank.

"I have to go out tonight. Do me a favor and pack some bags while I'm gone," Helen said.

"Are we going somewhere?"

"We are. Pack light. We can buy things we need when we get there. Pack some things for me, too, please."

"Where are we going, baby?"

Helen took two train tickets out of her pocket and handed them to Maria.

"New Orleans? How exciting!"

Helen smiled, though her body was tight with nerves. She loved to see Maria happy. She was looking forward to getting away with her.

"We leave early in the morning. I'll be home to get you and then we'll go catch the train."

"Where are you going tonight?" Maria asked.

"You don't want to know. I'll explain it all when we get on the train."

At ten thirty, the men drove Helen to The Haven. They went up to Clyde's apartment and found several men there already. There was plenty of drinking already going on.

"Nobody get too corked. I need you all to be alert and sharp when Moretti gets home."

Everyone was in good spirits. They all seemed to believe in Helen's plan. She was nervous and helped herself to a bourbon. Just a little something to calm the nerves, she told herself.

She pulled Jimmy aside.

"Hey, Jimmy. I'm going to get out of town as soon as this is over. I want you running the show for me while I'm gone."

"Where are you goin?"

"That's not important." Helen had decided no one but Maria would know where they disappeared to.

"Are you sure about this?"

"You ask me that a lot," Helen said. "And yes, I'm sure. You'll keep things running. But be careful. We'll all have targets on our back after this."

"I can do it. I appreciate the faith you have in me."

"Don't let me down."

The evening passed quickly and it got late fast. At just before three, Jimmy called from the window, "He's home!"

The group crowded by the front door. When they heard people in the hall, they stepped out and started shooting. Moretti's bodyguards crumpled.

Helen didn't take her aim off Moretti. She pumped him full of bullets and watched him dance as they riddled his body.

"That's it!" Helen called. "Everybody out!"

The men disbursed, and Helen's group rushed her back to her place. She quickly grabbed her suitcases and woke Maria up, who had dozed off waiting for her.

"Let's go, doll. Time to get out of here."

Helen's entourage dropped her at the train station untouched and she breathed a sigh of relief as the train pulled out of the station.

"So where were you tonight?" Maria asked, curled up against Helen in their car.

"I'd rather not talk about it right now." Helen was unsure what Maria's response would be to finding out she'd killed her longtime boyfriend.

"But you said you'd tell me when we got on the train."

"Let's just get some sleep tonight, and I'll tell you in the morning."

"Please tell me. I feel like you're too wound up to sleep anyway."

"That could be true." Helen laughed, knowing sleep was a long way away from her.

"And I got a nap, so I'm awake now, too. Plus now I'm worried. Why won't you tell me what you did?"

"I'm not sure how you're going to feel about it, doll. It was something I had to do, but I don't know that you'll see it that way."

"How could I not? If it was important to you, it will be important to me."

"Fine." Helen got up and looked out the door to make sure no one was within listening distance. Feeling safe, she said, "We took out Moretti tonight."

"You what? As in, you killed him?"

"Yes, Maria. As in, he's dead."

Maria sat silently and Helen felt the knot in her stomach grow. She'd known she'd have to tell Maria at some point, but had dreaded this moment.

"Maria?"

Maria just looked at her.

"I'm trying to absorb that," Maria said.

"How upset are you?" Helen asked.

"Upset? I'm not. I'm happy. It means you're safe from him now. But it hasn't quite sunk in."

"I'll never have to worry about Moretti again," Helen agreed. "However, Big Al will be after me for a long time now."

"So we'll be in New Orleans for a while, then?"

"A long while," Helen said.

"Can Al find us there?"

"Al can find us anywhere," Helen said. "But we'll have new identities there and we'll be laying low. I won't be conducting business. So we should be safe."

"New identities?"

"Yep. You'll be Diana D'Angelo and I'll be Grace Dunleavy."

"That's going to be hard to remember."

"Not when you consider our lives depend on it."

"That's true," Maria said. "Are you still too excited to sleep?"

"I think I am. Are you getting tired?"

"Not at all." Maria took Helen's hand and led her to bed.

She lay Helen on her back and unbuttoned her shirt, taking her time, drawing out the inevitable. She ran her hands over Helen's undershirt, stopping to tease the hard nipples underneath. She unbuttoned her slacks, then unzipped them, slowly pulling them down to her ankles. She slipped off her shoes and socks then finished removing the pants.

Helen was tense with anticipation. She arched her back to help Maria peel her underwear off. She lay exposed and aroused. Maria climbed between her legs and looked up at Helen. The passion in her eyes made Helen even wetter.

Maria loved Helen with her mouth and tongue, teasing her and pleasing her. Helen loved how Maria had grown into such a skilled lover. Tension from the night was replaced with tension of a different sort as her muscles contracted with the need for release.

As Maria continued to work her magic, Helen gripped the sheet as the orgasm tore through her. She wrapped her legs around Maria's head and squeezed.

Maria curled up next to Helen, and Helen realized how exhausted she was. They dozed together as the train made its way down the tracks to their new life.

Chapter Twenty-four

Helen and Maria, as Grace and Diana, stepped off the train in New Orleans. Helen hired a car to take them to the house she'd bought for them on Royal Street.

"This place is beautiful," Maria said. "I love it!"

"It's home," Helen said.

"I can't wait to furnish it."

"We can go shopping right now," Helen said. "Grace and Diana have plenty of money. We may as well use some of it on setting up a home."

"That sounds wonderful." Maria couldn't hide her excitement. Helen was pleased at how well Maria was doing.

"By the way," Helen said. "No one knows we're here. And no one can. I need to make sure you understand that."

"No one? Not even Jimmy?"

"Not even Jimmy."

"Well, I have no one in my life except you, so I won't be telling anyone. You don't need to worry about that."

"Good. Thank you."

They walked to a furniture store on Canal Street and Maria had the time of her life picking out chairs and tables and lamps. She picked an oak dining room set and Chippendale couch for the sitting room. She chose dark wing chairs also and oak end tables.

Helen found that she couldn't focus. She was looking at every person in the store and people down on the street, worried that somehow Capone's men may have found them. She tried to relax and share Maria's enthusiasm, but it wasn't happening. Every so often someone walked by and Helen swore it was someone from the South Side. She told herself she was being ridiculous, but she couldn't stop. Her fear was palpable.

"Baby, what's wrong?" Maria asked.

"Nothing, doll. I'm just keeping a lookout, is all."

"Why? You said yourself no one knows we're here. Relax. Come on. Let's pick out a bed."

The idea of picking out a bed to share with Maria made her pay more attention. This was something they would use for many nights to come. They made their way to the next floor and looked at the beds. They found a sleigh bed they both fell in love with.

"So I guess we've got everything we need, right, doll?"

"We still need dishes and pots and pans. Let's go find them."

Maria seemed to be having such a good time, Helen felt bad that she was so worried. But she just wanted to get back to the house and away from people who might recognize them, even as she told herself she was being unreasonable.

"Maybe we can get dishes another time," Helen said.

"Why wait? We're already here. Let's just buy them now."

Maria dragged Helen to the dishes and Helen participated in picking out a pattern they both loved. They bought pots and pans and then arranged to have everything delivered to their house. The bed would be delivered that night, and everything else over the next few days.

Helen was happy to be back at their house, empty though it was. It made her feel safe to be off the streets.

"Baby, are you okay?" Maria asked.

"I get nervous around all those people. What if someone saw us?"

"Who do we know in New Orleans? I know I don't know anybody. Do you?"

"No. But still. We can't be too sure."

"You're going to have to get used to being here. And being safe. We're safe. I truly believe that."

"I hope you're right," Helen said.

"What can I do to help you relax?" Maria rubbed her shoulders.

"I suppose I'll just have to learn to live without constant danger. It seems it won't be as easy as it sounds."

"Baby, I'm sorry. I wish it wasn't so hard for you. What do we need to do? Spend more time in public?"

"Or less."

Maria laughed. "We can't hide out in our courtyard forever."

"Let's go out there now. I like the courtyard."

Maria took Helen's hand, and together they walked to the slightly overgrown courtyard.

"I can't wait to work out here," Maria said. "This place is amazing."

Helen breathed deeply, inhaling the scents of the dock mingled with the fragrance of magnolias and wisteria. The dock was but a few blocks away and the scent of rotting bananas hung on the still of the air. The flowers bloomed on overgrown trees. The combination was heady and Helen marveled at the difference between New Orleans fresh air and that of Chicago.

The sounds were different, as well. Instead of the cacophony of sounds that assaulted her from the streets of Chicago, they heard jazz wafting their way.

It was a pleasant afternoon, and Helen relaxed in the comfort and safety of her new home. The knock at their door interrupted her reverie and she reached for her gun.

"Relax, baby," Maria said. "It's just the delivery guy, I'm sure."

Maria was right. They let the men in and directed them to the master bedroom. When the bed was assembled, Maria made it with their new linens while Helen tipped the workers. Helen came in just as Maria was finishing. She lay down on it, inhaling the fresh scent of their new home.

"This feels amazing," Helen said.

"Mind if I join you?" Helen extended her arm and Maria curled up next to her.

"Have I told you lately how much I love you?" Helen asked.

"I'm not sure. Maybe you should tell me again." Maria grinned.

Helen rolled onto her side and looked into Maria's eyes.

"I love you more than anything." She kissed her softly.

"And I love you, too," Maria said.

Helen kissed her again, this time prying her lips open with her tongue. Maria welcomed her tongue and Helen kissed her fervently, conveying her feelings through the kiss. She moved her hand to the front of Maria's blouse and deftly unbuttoned it. She ran her hand over the lacey lingerie underneath. She peeled the cup down and caressed the bare skin that sprung free.

Maria moaned into her mouth and Helen continued to gently squeeze her breast and tease her nipple. Helen got chills from Maria's reaction. She moved her hand down her soft belly and was frustrated when she reached the waistband of Maria's skirt. She reached around and fumbled with the button and zipper and finally pushed her skirt down and out of her way.

Helen dragged her fingers along the soft, moist crotch of Maria's panties, pressing them into her as she did. She moved the crotch to the side and ran her fingers through the thick wetness.

"You feel so good," Helen said.

"So do you."

Helen peeled the panties off and delved deep inside. She had forgotten her problems, her fears. All her focus was on pleasing Maria and the sensations that created in her. She felt alive, full of love for Maria. Maria surrounded her, engulfed her in their passion. She was completely caught up in the moment, feeling Maria closed tight around her.

Maria cried out as the first orgasm washed over her. Helen continued to please her until she screamed her name again.

Helen held Maria close as she floated back to the present.

"That was amazing, baby," Maria said.

"You're amazing, doll. I love you so much."

"I love you, too, but you're overdressed right now."

She unbuttoned Helen's shirt and untucked it. She trailed kisses everywhere her fingers touched, making Helen shiver with anticipation. Maria unfastened Helen's slacks and took them off, then straddled her and kissed her hard on her mouth. She kissed down her chest and sucked on an exposed nipple.

Helen's breasts were small but responsive. She felt them tighten as her clit swelled. She closed her eyes as Maria kissed down her stomach and pulled her underwear off with her teeth. She kissed the wet area she found underneath and Helen sucked in her breath.

She was getting lightheaded, losing her ability to think of anything except the impending burst of energy that was forming in her center. Maria made her feel things she didn't know she could, the pleasure far surpassing any she'd ever known.

When she could hold out no longer, Helen closed her eyes and rode the climax.

Maria climbed up next to her and snuggled into Helen's arms.

"I could get used to this living in New Orleans," Maria said.

"Good, because we're going to be here for a long time."

They dozed for a bit and woke up still tangled together.

"What should we do now?" Maria asked.

"I don't know about you, but I'm starving." Helen stretched.

"Mm. Food sounds good."

"I could use a cocktail first." Helen padded over to a suitcase that she had snuck in some bourbon.

"When did you pack that?"

"While we were trying to wake you up. I knew it might take a while until we're connected around here, so I brought some of my own. Would you like some?"

"You know I don't drink bourbon." Maria scrunched her nose. "Did you pack anything else?"

Helen withdrew a bottle of red wine.

"Does this look better?"

"Much. But, how are we going to drink this? We don't have any glasses."

Helen pulled out two glasses.

"You thought of everything."

"I tried."

"So where shall we go to dinner?"

"I heard of a couple restaurants down here that serve booze. I thought we could try one."

"Baby?" Maria looked worried.

"What's wrong?"

"Are you going to run booze down here, too?"

"No, doll. That was Helen Byrne. Grace Dunleavy isn't going to do that at all. We don't need the money. That's for sure."

"But won't you miss it?"

"Will I miss the power and the excitement? Sure. Will I miss being shot at every other day? No."

"Okay. I just worry that you'll get pulled into it again."

"Like you said, we're safe here. Let's keep it that way."

Chapter Twenty-five

Helen and Maria settled into their new lives with ease. They furnished their new home and christened every room. Things were going well, but Helen was getting restless.

"I need something to do, doll. I can't sit around the house all day."

"What do you want to do, baby?"

"Maybe I need to get a job."

"Helen, you've never held a job in your life. How do you think you'd get one now?"

"Maybe it wouldn't be a legit job."

"I thought you were through with a life of crime."

"I'm through running booze." She was silent for a moment. "You're right. I don't want a life of crime. But what other kind of job could I get?"

"Maybe we should travel," Maria suggested. "We've got the money. That way you wouldn't feel stuck in a rut."

"That's only temporary. I need to do something."

"Why don't you start a legit business?"

"Doing what?"

"I don't know. What interests you?"

"I wish I could open a bar. I wish Prohibition would end. I never thought I'd say that, but now that I'm a solid citizen, it would be nice to have a bar or restaurant and bar."

"Let's go for a walk," Maria said. "Maybe something will jump out at you."

They walked over to Bourbon Street and looked at the businesses there.

"I could open a place that sells cigars," Helen mused.

"That would never work," Maria said.

They walked on, crossing Canal Street and taking in the activity of the bustling city. They turned on to Common Street and saw a vacant lot with a for sale sign.

"I wonder what will be built here," Maria said.

"A hotel," Helen said. "A fine, luxurious hotel. With themes of New Orleans all through it."

Maria stopped and stared at her, the dreamy tone of her voice making her pause.

"How do you know that?"

"Don't you see? This is what I can do. I can build a hotel!"

"Are you sure?"

"I'm positive! I'll build a fancy hotel that will be the talk of the country. People will come from all over to stay at my hotel!"

"I haven't seen you this excited since we got here," Maria said. "Maybe this is something you really should do."

Helen committed the phone number to memory and they hurried back to their house. As soon as they got there, Helen dialed the number.

As businesswoman Grace Dunleavy, she ironed out the details with the realtor and hung up the phone.

"Now all I need to do is build the hotel," she told Maria.

❖

Construction took the better part of a year, and finally, a classy hotel stood in the once vacant lot. The white marble façade welcomed visitors, and the two hundred plus rooms offered them a luxurious place to stay. Each floor celebrated a jazz player, and the work of local photographers lined the walls.

The grand opening was attended by many of New Orleans' dignitaries. Grace Dunleavy was looked at as an up and coming businesswoman in the city. She knew all eyes were on her as she and Maria greeted their guests in the Creole-styled dining room of the hotel's restaurant.

They served raw oysters, duck and andouille sausage gumbo, and seared steak. The people ate and enjoyed themselves even though there was no alcohol served.

The night was a success and half the rooms in the hotel were filled.

"Not a bad way to start a new business," Maria said.

Helen escorted her upstairs to their suite at the top of the hotel. She had a bootlegged bottle of champagne on ice in the sitting room. She took her coat off and filled the glasses, handing one to Maria.

"Here's to a successful hotel," Maria said.

"Here's to us," Helen said.

They clinked their glasses together and drank. Helen was still excited from the night. She lit a cigar and sat in a chair, looking at Maria.

"Tonight went beautifully," Maria said. "I'm so proud of you."

"Thanks, doll. I'm pretty proud of myself."

"You should be. This hotel is amazing. And you worked so hard for it. I'm so glad you found a real business you could get excited about."

"I worry about people from Chicago coming to stay here," Helen said.

"So what if they do? You'll be working behind the scenes mostly, doing the books and making sure things run well. No one will need to see you."

"Still, what if they do?"

"You're worrying for no reason." Maria stood behind Helen and rubbed her shoulders.

"That feels great." Helen leaned back into Maria. She set her cigar down and sipped her champagne.

"You need to relax," Maria said. "You've worked like a dog for the past year getting this place open. Just relax and enjoy your success."

"I'm thinking more about relaxing and enjoying you right now."

"I like the sound of that."

She continued to massage her and Helen felt the tension of her worries melting away.

"Your touch is like heaven."

Maria leaned forward to kiss Helen's cheek, her firm breasts pressing against Helen's shoulders. Helen felt the familiar stir in her crotch. She turned her head and took Maria's lips with hers.

Maria kissed her back, and Helen soon forgot her worries as she arched in to kiss her harder.

Helen stood and took Maria in her arms. She held her tight and ran her hand along her back, down to cup her shapely ass.

"I love you, doll."

"I love you, baby."

She kissed her again, softly at first. The kiss grew more intense as their tongues met and danced together over each other. She pulled Maria closer, feeling her body pressing against her and grew dizzy with need.

"You're more beautiful now than when I met you," Helen murmured.

Maria responded by kissing her more passionately. Helen felt Maria's nipples poking through her dress. She dropped a hand and teased one. Maria moaned into her mouth. Helen kissed her fervently and squeezed her breast.

"Let's get you out of this dress," Helen whispered. She spun Maria around and unzipped her. When the dress hit the floor, she unhooked her bra and tossed it onto the dress. She cupped her breasts and bent to kiss the top of one, then the other.

"You have the most perfect breasts," she breathed.

Maria held Helen's shoulders to steady herself. Helen took a nipple in her mouth and ran her tongue lovingly over it. She felt Maria's intake of breath and grew more aroused. She loved knowing Maria wanted her.

Helen felt Maria's grip tighten and moved to the other nipple. She sucked it deep and flicked the tip with her tongue.

Maria pulled Helen upright and unbuttoned her shirt. She pushed it off her shoulders and dropped it onto the pile of clothes. She pulled her undershirt off and wrapped her arms around her.

Helen grew wetter at the feel of skin on skin. Maria was so soft. Her skin was like silk to Helen's touch. She rubbed her hands all over her, memorizing anew every inch of her. She kissed her again as she slipped her hand under Maria's panties.

Maria grabbed her wrist and pulled her hand out, stepping out of her underwear as she did. She stood naked, save for her garters and stockings. Helen was crazy with desire. She wanted all of her and she wanted her at that moment.

Maria stepped back and unbuttoned Helen's slacks, letting them fall to the floor. She peeled off her boxers and led her to the bed. She sat Helen down and took her socks off, leaving her bare for her. She pushed her back and lay on top of her. Helen took her in her arms and rolled over, pinning Maria under her.

Helen kissed her again while she brought her knee up to press it into Maria's center. She moved her hand to Maria's breast and fondled it.

"I can't get enough of you," Helen said.

"I can't get enough of you," Maria agreed.

Helen suckled at Maria's breast for a long while before kissing down her belly and finding where she needed to be between her legs. She lapped at the juices flowing there, relishing the taste of Maria. The more she licked, the more juices came and Helen was again amazed at Maria's response to her.

She sucked her lips and ran her tongue over her. She moved her mouth to Maria's swollen clit and drew it between her lips. She could feel it pulsing with need. She sucked on it until she felt Maria tense up, pressing her face into her as she reached orgasm.

Helen stayed put until Maria was completely relaxed, then she kissed her way back up her body and pulled her close.

"You make me feel so good," Maria said as she caught her breath. "My turn now."

She kissed Helen and moved her hand between Helen's legs. Helen was wet with desire. She spread her legs wider to allow Maria easier access. She felt Maria's fingers stroking her and closed her eyes, lost in the feelings. Maria teased Helen's clit, dragging her fingers over it and making it grow even more. She buried her fingers inside Helen and Helen got wetter yet, enjoying feeling full.

Maria moved her fingers in and out as Helen bucked against her. She writhed on the sheet, arching to take more of Maria. She took her deeper and deeper until she could take no more. She cried out as she vaulted into the climax, her body shaking in its power.

Helen opened her arms and Maria climbed next to her, holding her close. They fell into a deep sleep with Helen dreaming of their wonderful new life.

Epilogue

Seven years had passed since the opening of the hotel. It was a huge success, always filled close to capacity. Helen wondered frequently how things were in Chicago. She followed the news and was glad she hadn't been there when the St. Valentine's Day Massacre happened, but cheered with Maria when Capone had finally been arrested. Helen still worried that someone from Chicago would book a room at the hotel, but so far, it hadn't happened.

Winter nipped at Helen and Maria as they walked along Bourbon Street one afternoon in early December. Helen laughed at herself, thinking that she was ridiculous to feel cold. December in New Orleans was nothing like December in Chicago. She smiled to herself, realizing that she had acclimated and settled in to her new life.

It was December fourth and Prohibition had finally been repealed. They stopped by places they'd avoided the past eight years, since they'd become law-abiding citizens. But now it was legal to drink again, and they enjoyed it with all the other revelers. After a couple of hours of drinking, they walked to the hotel for the shipment that Helen had arranged to arrive just before the dinner hour.

When they arrived at the hotel, they found a crowd had already gathered. They were greeted by cheers as they explained the booze would be arriving any moment. Helen was surprised to find the place so crowded. She hadn't expected people to come there when they heard about the twenty-first amendment passing. She hadn't given her regular customers enough credit.

The liquor was flowing as soon as it was off the truck. Helen's customers were thirsty for legal alcohol and they'd come to the right place. If that evening was any indication, Helen was about to increase her cash flow significantly.

The next day, Helen started construction on a bar next to the restaurant. She supervised the building of it, and soon it was open for business. The night it opened, they featured Johnny Breaux and the Jazz Kings. She hadn't been this happy since the days when she ran the speakeasies in Chicago. She found that, while she enjoyed being a businesswoman very much, her love was in running bars.

The bar, called The Speakeasy, opened every morning at ten and always had a crowd by noon. People would come in and drink then have lunch in the restaurant. Cocktail hour started at three, and local business people started stopping by before heading home for the day.

Helen still did the books for the hotel, as well as the restaurant and bar. She oversaw the running of the hotel, as well. No one was hired or fired without her say. Grace Dunleavy was known as a fair, but formidable employer. She was at work early every morning and stayed until five o'clock every evening. At precisely five o'clock every day, Diana D'Angelo walked into the bar and Grace would step out from her office and join Diana for a drink. Regulars were used to the routine and looked forward to seeing them together. It was part of a routine they'd all grown accustomed to.

After the drink, they walked back to the house for supper and a relaxing evening together. Life was good for Helen. She couldn't believe how well she'd done for herself legally.

"Hey, doll," she said one night to Maria.

"What, baby?"

"You ever think that maybe we should go back to Chicago and see how people are doing?"

"No. That's part of our past. It's not part of our present."

"But Capone's in prison. Who's going to hurt us?"

"We don't know. I'm sure your face has been burned into the memories of all his people. They wouldn't think twice about killing you the minute they laid eyes on you."

Helen wasn't convinced. "I doubt it. I'm sure I'm long forgotten by now. I'm serious, Maria. Wouldn't it be nice to see how Jimmy and the guys are?"

"It's not worth it," Maria persisted.

"But with Prohibition over, the gangs are probably all disbursed. I doubt they exist any longer. It's probably never been safer."

"Are you kidding me?" Maria asked. "I'm sure they've just switched to other illegal activities. Those gangs aren't going anywhere."

Helen let out a heavy sigh. She knew Maria was right, but she missed Jimmy and the gang. She didn't even know if they were still alive. For all she knew, Capone had had them all killed after they took out Moretti. She longed to go to Chicago to see for herself. But she knew Maria had the right idea. She probably still had a target on her and likely always would.

Maria crossed the room and took Helen's hand.

"I know a way to get your mind off Chicago," she said.

Helen stood and followed Maria to the bedroom, where the only thing that mattered was them. In the here and now.

About the Author

MJ Williamz, author of the award winning novel *Initiation By Desire*, was raised on California's Central Coast, which she still loves, but left at the age of seventeen to pursue an education. She graduated from Chico State with a degree in business management. It was in Chico that MJ began to pursue her love of writing.

Now living in Portland, Oregon, MJ has made writing an integral part of her life. Since 2002, she's had over thirty short stories published, mostly erotica with a few romance thrown in for good measure. *Speakeasy* is MJ's fourth novel.

Books Available from Bold Strokes Books

Timeless by Rachel Spangler. When Stevie Geller returns to her hometown, will she do things differently the second time around or will she be in such a hurry to leave her past that she misses out on a better future? (978-1-62639-050-8)

Second to None by L.T. Marie. Can a physical therapist and a custom motorcycle designer conquer their pasts and build a future with one another? (978-1-62639-051-5)

Seneca Falls by Jesse Thoma. Together, two women discover love truly can conquer all evil. (978-1-62639-052-2)

A Kingdom Lost by Barbara Ann Wright. Without knowing each other's fate, Princess Katya and her consort Starbride seek to reclaim their kingdom from the magic-wielding madman who seized the throne and is murdering their people. (978-1-62639-053-9)

Uncommon Romance by Jove Belle. Sometimes sex is just sex, and sometimes it's the only way to say "I love you." (978-1-62639-057-7)

The Heat of Angels by Lisa Girolami. Fires burn in more than one place in Los Angeles. (978-1-62639-042-3)

Season of the Wolf by Robin Summers. Two women running from their pasts are thrust together by an unimaginable evil. Can they overcome the horrors that haunt them in time to save each other? (978-1-62639-043-0)

Desperate Measures by P. J. Trebelhorn. Homicide detective Kay Griffith and contractor Brenda Jansen meet amidst turmoil neither of them is aware of until murder suspect Tommy Rayne makes his move to exact revenge on Kay. (978-1-62639-044-7)

The Magic Hunt by L.L. Raand. With her Pack being hunted by human extremists and beset by enemies masquerading as friends, can Sylvan protect them and her mate, or will she succumb to the feral rage that threatens to turn her rogue, destroying them all? A Midnight Hunters novel. (978-1-62639-045-4)

Waiting for the Violins by Justine Saracen. After surviving Dunkirk, a scarred and embittered British nurse returns to Nazi-occupied Brussels to join the Resistance, and finds that nothing is fair in love and war. (978-1-62639-046-1)

Because of Her by KE Payne. When Tabby Morton is forced to move to London, she's convinced her life will never be the same again. But the beautiful and intriguing Eden Palmer is about to show her that this time, change is most definitely for the better. (978-1-62639-049-2)

Wingspan by Karis Walsh. Wildlife biologist Bailey Chase is content to live at the wild bird sanctuary she has created on Washington's Olympic Peninsula until she is lured beyond the safety of isolation by architect Kendall Pearson. (978-1-60282-983-1)

Tumbledown by Cari Hunter. After surviving their ordeal in the North Cascades, Alex and Sarah have new identities and a new home, but a chance occurrence threatens everything: their freedom and their lives. (978-1-62639-085-0)

Night Bound by Winter Pennington. Kass struggles to keep her head, her heart, and her relationships in order. She's still having a difficult time accepting being an Alpha female. But her wolf is certain of what she wants and she's intent on securing her power. (978-1-60282-984-8)

Slash and Burn by Valerie Bronwen. The murder of a roundly despised author at an LGBT writer's conference in New Orleans turns Winter Lovelace's relaxing weekend hobnobbing with her peers into a nightmare of suspense—especially when her ex turns up. (978-1-60282-986-2)

The Blush Factor by Gun Brooke. Ice-cold business tycoon Eleanor Ashcroft only cares about the three P's—Power, Profit, and Prosperity—until young Addison Garr makes her doubt both that and the state of her frostbitten heart. (978-1-60282-985-5)

The Quickening: A Sisters of Spirits Novel by Yvonne Heidt. Ghosts, visions, and demons are all in a day's work for Tiffany. But when Kat asks for help on a serial killer case, life takes on another dimension altogether. (978-1-60282-975-6)

Windigo Thrall by Cate Culpepper. Six women trapped in a mountain cabin by a blizzard, stalked by an ancient cannibal demon bent on stealing their sanity—and their lives. (978-1-60282-950-3)

Smoke and Fire by Julie Cannon. Oil and water, passion and desire, a combustible combination. Can two women fight the fire that draws them together and threatens to keep them apart? (978-1-60282-977-0)

Asher's Fault by Elizabeth Wheeler. Fourteen-year-old Asher Price sees the world in black and white, much like the photos he takes, but when his little brother drowns at the same moment Asher experiences his first same-sex kiss, he can no longer hide behind the lens of his camera and eventually discovers he isn't the only one with a secret. (978-1-60282-982-4)

Love and Devotion by Jove Belle. KC Hall trips her way through life, stumbling into an affair with a married bombshell twice her age. Thankfully, her best friend, Emma Reynolds, is there to show her the true meaning of Love and Devotion. (978-1-60282-965-7)

Rush by Carsen Taite. Murder, secrets, and romance combine to create the ultimate rush. (978-1-60282-966-4)

The Shoal of Time by J.M. Redmann. It sounded too easy. Micky Knight is reluctant to take the case because the easy ones often turn into the hard ones, and the hard ones turn into the dangerous ones. In this one, easy turns hard without warning. (978-1-60282-967-1)

In Between by Jane Hoppen. At the age of 14, Sophie Schmidt discovers that she was born an intersexual baby and sets off on a journey to find her place in a world that denies her true existence. (978-1-60282-968-8)

Secret Lies by Amy Dunne. While fleeing from her abuser, Nicola Jackson bumps into Jenny O'Connor, and their unlikely friendship quickly develops into a blossoming romance—but when it comes down to a matter of life or death, are they both willing to face their fears? (978-1-60282-970-1)

Under Her Spell by Maggie Morton. The magic of love brought Terra and Athene together, but now a magical quest stands between them—a quest for Athene's hand in marriage. Will their passion keep them together, or will stronger magic tear them apart? (978-1-60282-973-2)

Homestead by Radclyffe. R. Clayton Sutter figures getting NorthAm Fuel's newest refinery operational on a rolling tract of land in Upstate New York should take a month or two, but then, she hadn't counted on local resistance in the form of vandalism, petitions, and one furious farmer named Tess Rogers. (978-1-60282-956-5)

Battle of Forces: Sera Toujours by Ali Vali. Kendal and Piper return to New Orleans to start the rest of eternity together, but the return of an old enemy makes their peaceful reunion short-lived, especially when they join forces with the new queen of the vampires. (978-1-60282-957-2)

How Sweet It Is by Melissa Brayden. Some things are better than chocolate. Molly O'Brien enjoys her quiet life running the bakeshop in a small town. When the beautiful Jordan Tuscana returns home, Molly can't deny the attraction—or the stirrings of something more. (978-1-60282-958-9)

The Missing Juliet: A Fisher Key Adventure by Sam Cameron. A teenage detective and her friends search for a kidnapped Hollywood star in the Florida Keys. (978-1-60282-959-6)

Amor and More: Love Everafter edited by Radclyffe and Stacia Seaman. Rediscover favorite couples as Bold Strokes

Books authors reveal glimpses of life and love beyond the honeymoon in short stories featuring main characters from favorite BSB novels. (978-1-60282-963-3)

First Love by CJ Harte. Finding true love is hard enough, but for Jordan Thompson, daughter of a conservative president, it's challenging, especially when that love is a female rodeo cowgirl. (978-1-60282-949-7)

Pale Wings Protecting by Lesley Davis. Posing as a couple to investigate the abduction of infants, Special Agent Blythe Kent and Detective Daryl Chandler find themselves drawn into a battle over the innocents, with demons on one side and the unlikeliest of protectors on the other. (978-1-60282-964-0)

Mounting Danger by Karis Walsh. Sergeant Rachel Bryce, an outcast on the police force, is put in charge of the department's newly formed mounted division. Can she and polo champion Callan Lanford resist their growing attraction as they struggle to safeguard the disaster-prone unit? (978-1-60282-951-0)

Meeting Chance by Jennifer Lavoie. When man's best friend turns on Aaron Cassidy, the teen keeps his distance until fate puts Chance in his hands. (978-1-60282-952-7)

At Her Feet by Rebekah Weatherspoon. Digital marketing producer Suzanne Kim knows she has found the perfect love in her new mistress Pilar, but before they can make the ultimate commitment, Suzanne's professional life threatens to disrupt their perfectly balanced bliss. (978-1-60282-948-0)

Show of Force by AJ Quinn. A chance meeting between navy pilot Evan Kane and correspondent Tate McKenna takes them on a roller-coaster ride where the stakes are high, but the reward is higher: a chance at love. (978-1-60282-942-8)

Clean Slate by Andrea Bramhall. Can Erin and Morgan work through their individual demons to rediscover their love for each other, or are the unexplainable wounds too deep to heal? (978-1-60282-943-5)

Hold Me Forever by D. Jackson Leigh. An investigation into illegal cloning in the quarter horse racing industry threatens to destroy the growing attraction between Georgia debutante Mae St. John and Louisiana horse trainer Whit Casey. (978-1-60282-944-2)

Trusting Tomorrow by PJ Trebelhorn. Funeral director Logan Swift thinks she's perfectly happy with her solitary life devoted to helping others cope with loss until Brooke Collier moves in next door to care for her elderly grandparents. (978-1-60282-891-9)

Forsaking All Others by Kathleen Knowles. What if what you think you want is the opposite of what makes you happy? (978-1-60282-892-6)

Exit Wounds by VK Powell. When Officer Loane Landry falls in love with ATF informant Abigail Mancuso, she realizes that nothing is as it seems—not the case, not her lover, not even the dead. (978-1-60282-893-3)